Christmas Secrets
in Snowflake Cove

EMILY HARVALE

Emily Harvale lives in East Sussex, in the UK – although she would prefer to live in the French Alps…or Canada…or anywhere that has several months of snow. Emily loves snow almost as much as she loves Christmas.

Having worked in the City (London) for several years, Emily returned to her home town of Hastings where she spends her days writing. And wondering if it will snow.

You can contact her via her website, Twitter, Facebook or Instagram.

There is also a Facebook group where fans can chat with Emily about her books, her writing day and life in general. Details are on the 'For You' page of Emily's website.

Author contacts:
www.emilyharvale.com
www.twitter.com/emilyharvale
www.facebook.com/emilyharvalewriter
www.instagram.com/emilyharvale

***

Scan the code above to see all Emily's books on Amazon

Also by this author:

Highland Fling
Lizzie Marshall's Wedding
The Golf Widows' Club
Sailing Solo
Carole Singer's Christmas
Christmas Wishes – Two short stories
A Slippery Slope
The Perfect Christmas Plan – A novella
Be Mine – A novella
***

The Goldebury Bay series:
Book One – Ninety Days of Summer
Book Two – Ninety Steps to Summerhill
Book Three – Ninety Days to Christmas
***

The Hideaway Down series:
Book One – A Christmas Hideaway
Book Two – Catch A Falling Star
Book Three – Walking on Sunshine
Book Four – Dancing in the Rain
***

Hall's Cross series
Deck the Halls
The Starlight Ball

Christmas Secrets

in

Snowflake Cove

Emily Harvale

ISBN 978-1-909917-27-9

Published by Crescent Gate Publishing

Print edition published worldwide 2017
E-edition published worldwide 2017

Editor Christina Harkness

Cover design by JR, Luke Brabants and Emily Harvale

This book is dedicated to all the lovely members of Emily Harvale's Readers' Club – that's all the subscribers to my Readers' Club newsletter and the members of my exclusive, Readers' Club Facebook group. Here's to a very Merry Christmas for all of you, and to lots more fun, laughter and general silliness in the future. You're all stars and I am so, so grateful to each and every one of you for your constant friendship and support.

Acknowledgements

My grateful thanks go to the following:

Christina Harkness for her patience and care in editing this book.
My webmaster, David Cleworth who does so much more than website stuff.
My cover design team, JR.
Luke Brabants. Luke is a talented artist and can be found at: www.lukebrabants.com
My wonderful friends for their friendship and love. You know I love you all.
All the fabulous members of my Readers' Club. You help and support me in so many ways and I am truly grateful for your ongoing friendship. I wouldn't be where I am today without you.
My Twitter and Facebook friends, and fans of my Facebook author page. It's great to chat with you. You help to keep me (relatively) sane!
Thank you for buying this book.

Christmas Secrets

in

Snowflake Cove

Chapter One

Evie Starr eased open the blackened-oak front door of Snowflake Inn and smiled. Were things finally taking a turn for the better? Had her dad been right all along when he said that it would all sort itself out by Christmas? Christmas was a time for miracles and magic and the Big Day was less than a week away. Had it already started sprinkling its magic dust over the tiny village of Snowflake Cove?

Her gran, Jessie Starr was always the first to know everything concerning Snowflake Cove and its much larger neighbour, Michaelmas Bay, so there was no reason to doubt the news. If Jessie said Zachary Thorn was bringing his TV show to town – he was. And that was an opportunity not to be missed. This could be the gift that kept on giving. The answer to all their problems. With any luck.

Evie struggled to contain her excitement as the centuries-old hinges of the door creaked and groaned. Her gran had made similar sounding protests a few minutes earlier when Evie told her that her help was required in the kitchen. That meant she had to move from her armchair beside one of the inn's three, roaring log fires.

'Things are grim,' Jessie said, making it clear that getting to her feet required considerable effort, 'when an eighty-eight-year-old still has to work for her bed and board. Life in the workhouse would have been a holiday compared to living here.'

Jessie Starr might be getting on in years but she was as fit as a fiddle. If Evie had a penny for each time she heard that statement, the Starr family wouldn't have any money worries. And they wouldn't need to get Zachary Thorn on their side.

'I know, Gran. Mum and Dad have no pity. But how can Mum make Jessie Starr's famous shortbread and mince pies without the help of the one and only, star baker – Jessie Starr herself?'

Jessie grinned at her. 'You've got a silver tongue, my girl. I thought you, your father and Raven were going to check outside. If the roof survived last night's storm intact, I'll be surprised, let alone those lights. You want that whippersnapper Thorn to see this place at its best, don't you? Not much point in getting him here in the hope of drumming up business if there's no roof on the inn. What are you waiting for?

Christmas?'

Evie smiled and bent to kiss her. Despite the warmth from the fire, Jessie's ivory complexion didn't have a hint of redness on her tissue-like skin and it was cool against Evie's lips, like filo pastry taken from the fridge and rolled over porcelain bones. 'On my way, Gran.'

Evie had a great many things to do if the Starrs were going to 'shine' on TV screens all over the planet. OK, perhaps the planet was a bit of an exaggeration, but Zachary's live TV show: 'Thorn On Your Side' was one of the most-watched primetime shows, according to the rankings. The play on words for the title was a bit crass, but if anything, it seemed to attract viewers rather than put them off. So many shows were about making fun of people or exposing a person's worst traits or getting them to compete for some coveted prize like inept gladiators in a Big-Screen version of an amphitheatre. Zachary's show wasn't like that. It was about helping people achieve their goals, which ranged from starting a business to overcoming a phobia of some kind, by giving them advice and support. Negativity was banned and viewers were left with a feel-good factor, not baying for blood, figuratively speaking. Everyone in Snowflake Cove watched it. Not that that counted for many. There only thirty-eight permanent residents in the tiny village, including the Starr family – although technically they lived on Snowflake Isle. But despite the fact that the inn sat on a miniscule island, two hundred or so metres from the mainland, it was connected to it by a long, narrow wooden bridge and had always been part of Snowflake Cove.

'We must get this door fixed, Dad,' Evie said, as she stepped outside. 'I'm always worried the hinges will snap, they're so ancient. Shall I add it to my list, or yours?'

'It's already on my list but I'll move it nearer to the top.'

A shaft of light streamed past from the reception area, dappling the rain-soaked cobbles with a golden glow and turning puddles on the path into liquid caramel. Evie glanced behind her to smile at her dad – and splashed straight into one. Thank heavens she had worn boots rather than shoes. The water level settled above her ankles.

'Mind that–' Her dad, John Starr hadn't been so sensible, but her warning came too late. She shook her head and tutted as he peered down at his submerged, brown leather lace-ups, pulling a face when, no doubt, the ice-cold rainwater began seeping in. 'I told you to put your wellies on.'

'Drat,' he said, hanging his head like a naughty child. He shook one leg after the other and found a few puddle-free cobbles to stand on before grinning at her. 'Dry land. This'll be like playing hopscotch when I was a kid, except with puddles instead of numbers.'

Evie couldn't help but return his grin. John Starr was well known for his knack of being able

4

to see a bright side to everything. He could even see a light amongst the Starr's financial worries. Or perhaps he was simply putting on a brave face whenever any of the family tried to discuss the problem by reassuring them that things weren't that bad and that it would all sort itself out by Christmas.

Evie had doubted that – until today. With the festive season already underway and Christmas Day less than a week away, the future hadn't looked particularly bright for the Starrs. Her gran's news about Zachary Thorn was a beacon of hope.

'At least we still have a roof over our heads,' John said, as if reading her mind. 'Or I hope we do. This TV thing could be just what the doctor ordered.' He winked at Evie and turned his attention to the roof to search for missing tiles and any other signs of damage.

'I hope so. I'll take a look at the lights, and Raven … Raven?' Evie tilted her head to look past her dad and back inside towards the reception in search of her fifteen-year-old niece. 'Where's she gone? She was right behind us.'

'She's probably flown the nest.' Chuckling at his little joke, he gave Evie a brief hug and ambled away, every now and then hopping over a puddle before splashing into another. He hummed 'White Christmas', got it mixed up with 'I Saw Three Ships' and ended up with something unrecognisable. But at least it sounded jolly.

Evie wished she could be more like him and

not worry so much about everything, but at thirty-four, there was no chance of changing the habits of a lifetime. She was one of life's worriers and that was that.

The front door was wide open and Evie turned back to close it to keep the heat from escaping. Roaring log fires in the reception area, lounge, dining room and bar made Snowflake Inn feel like the tropics, but a few minutes of an open door or window and the temperature would soon start to drop. The storm may have abated since last night but bitter winds still blew in from the hills to the north of Snowflake Cove and whistled their way through Michaelmas Great Wood. Earlier, Jessie had insisted she could smell snow in the air. That was all they needed. It had been an atrocious summer with little sunshine. Autumn brought more rain and with it came several storms, so bad that the Met Office had given them names. A winter of snow and blizzards, they could definitely do without.

Evie let out a long, low sigh. She couldn't worry about snow right now. She had far too many other things to think about. A long list of things. And Raven was supposed to be helping. Where was she?

Perhaps her niece had indeed flown the nest and was heading to the train station in Michaelmas Bay instead of standing out here freezing to death. Evie shivered as the wind found its way to an exposed area of her neck and bit her freckled skin.

She wrapped her scarf tighter. The quicker she checked the lights, the sooner she'd be back inside, warming herself by the fire and breathing in the spices her mum and gran would be using to make Jessie Starr's famous shortbread and mince pies.

That's probably where Raven was. She had been right behind Evie a few minutes earlier. She'd probably headed to the kitchen instead of coming outside. And who could blame her? Ice crystals were forming around the edges of the puddles. Great. Another thing Evie would need to add to the list. The entire path from the front door to the bridge linking Snowflake Isle to the mainland would need to be covered with grit and sand. They didn't have many guests – only two at the moment – but they couldn't take any chances on someone slipping on ice and breaking their hip or something. And if Evie could find a way to get Zachary Thorn and his TV crew to visit Snowflake Inn, knowing her family's luck, it would probably be the man himself who took a tumble. The Starrs would have a law suit to add to their growing pile of debt.

An image of Zachary Thorn lying injured in her bed, his long honey blond eyelashes fluttering against his tanned cheeks, his equally bronzed, bare chest rising and falling dramatically, his strong arms resting atop her snowman-covered Christmas duvet, made her smile even though it shouldn't. Quite why the handsome hunk was in her bed and not in one of the guest bedrooms – or in hospital – was a mystery to Evie, and he wouldn't be half-naked if he had any sense. Despite all the other bedrooms being kept at the ideal temperature thanks to the back boilers served by one of the fires and the aged Aga, the radiator in her bedroom had a mind of its own. It veered between stone-cold and tepid. The man would freeze to death if he didn't wear pyjamas.

Somehow, she couldn't quite envision Zachary Thorn in Christmas-themed PJs. Her family all wore Christmas themed nightclothes during the festive season which, in the Starr household, began on the day the first chocolate was taken from each of their advent calendars. Chocolate-filled advent calendars were another Starr family tradition.

She could offer to keep him warm. Kissing him better had great appeal. But that particular dream would never come true and besides, Zachary wouldn't let a few broken bones keep him down. He was ex-SAS. Even his honey blond hair was trying to escape beneath the bandages swathed about his head in her imaginary scenario. He'd no doubt had more injuries than she'd had hot water bottles, and been in far colder places than her bedroom. She probably had more chance of joining the SAS herself than she did of sharing passionate kisses with Zachary Thorn. Her wild, ginger hair and a face splattered with freckles wouldn't be Zachary's idea of attractive. The man had women falling at his feet. He was drop-dead gorgeous. He was also a bit of an enigma, which added to the attraction.

His career in the British Army special forces ended a little over a year ago after a 'classified incident' about which no one knew the facts, other than that a man under his command had been 'lost' during a training exercise and Zachary resigned his commission as a result. But his act of heroism in saving several people's lives after an horrific, freak accident in London a few months later had set him on the unlikely career path of a TV presenter. His Adonis-like looks ensured he would have a glowing future on the small screen. Everyone loves a hero, and any previous 'grey areas' in his past were quickly forgiven and forgotten. Evie, along with half the population, would love to know the facts, but Zachary was a man of secrets and for once the media didn't seem interested in delving into them, classified or not. At least for the time being.

She cleared her mind of him – or tried to, and typed the words sand and grit into her phone and on to her ever-growing list. If the plan worked, Snowflake Inn would soon be heaving with people and the old wooden bridge crossing would be bowing under the weight.

Oh God. What if it collapsed? The narrow channel of water separating the isle from the mainland was about an eighth of a mile wide, if that, but it was like one of those fast water rides in theme parks. When the tide came in, the rush of water could sweep people right around the isle like bobbing ducks at the fair, pushing them into any number of tiny inlets and bumping them into the sharp, sloping rocks of the snowflake-shaped isle, before carrying them into the wide, tidal waters of Michaelmas Bay. The natural rock harbour there, would offer shelter, but some poor souls could be washed through the gap and out to sea.

Why on earth was she worrying about that? That kind of thing only happened in disaster movies. It was technically possible but most unlikely. She really needed to concentrate and not get carried away on these flights of fancy. How had she gone from picturing Zachary in her bed, to seeing people drowning? Oh yes... a rather over-active imagination and a tendency to worry about things that will never happen.

She raised her eyes skywards. Another storm was on the way and it looked like rain or hail if the charcoal-grey clouds were anything to go by. At least there was plenty of wood for the fires. One advantage of living in Snowflake Cove was that Michaelmas Bay harbour virtually wrapped itself around the cove and the isle, thereby protecting them from the worst of the weather. Another was the fact that Michaelmas Great Wood was common land. It came with ancient rights for residents to 'take wood for their fires' – and that included the owners of Snowflake Inn. That meant one less bill to worry about.

At the beginning of the year, her dad had decided it would be a good idea to have solar panels fitted to provide electricity. Great, in theory. Not so good in reality. Due to the fact the building was Grade II listed and the roof was clearly visible both from land and sea, so as not to 'detract from its authenticity', the panels had to be set up on the ground, at vast expense, a short distance from the inn. But the sun had been noticeable by its absence this year and in spite of the panels resembling a mini, NASA array, Evie doubted there was enough energy stored to see the Starrs through this winter. She hoped for an early spring, because if the forecasters were to be believed, the next few months would bring nothing but rain, cloud, and for the rest of December, snow, snow and more snow. She loved snow, but it made things even more difficult as far as running the inn was concerned.

The only access to Snowflake Inn was via the old wooden bridge and although it was solid, it was narrow. Too narrow for cars to cross. In any event there was no place for a car park on Snowflake Isle. The footprint of the inn took up most of it. Only the inn, the sun terrace and gardens on the part facing Michaelmas Bay, and the cobbled path and lawn at the front of the inn, stood on level ground. The rest of the isle consisted of sloping banks, jagged rocks and sandy inlets. During exceptionally high tides – of which there had been a few this year – the sea came within metres of the ancient, wattle and daub, timber framed building. Even if an area could be flattened for a car park, there was a distinct possibility of the vehicles being surrounded by water at such times. No one wanted that. Not that the Starrs could afford to build a car park. The last of their savings had been sunk into the solar panels.

The Starrs did not own a car but Evie's dad roared around on a motorbike. It was almost as old as him and was kept in the small stable-come-shed-come-wood store attached to the inn. To ferry guests from the mainland to the isle they still used the method adopted many centuries before: a horse and a long, narrow, covered cart with seats on only one side. Most guests found this mode of transport exciting, romantic, or at least, quirky, but some took an instant dislike to it and preferred to walk, moaning the entire way. That irritated Evie. It was clear on the website that the inn was on a little isle, joined to the mainland by a bridge. It was also made clear how guests would get across. It seemed some people couldn't read. Admittedly, it was described as a 'short but scenic carriage ride', but the photos showed exactly what the 'carriage' looked like, both inside and out.

A few moments after Evie had shut the front door, it burst open and Raven, dressed from head to toe in black – black combat boots, black jeans, black jumper, long black coat, black hoody – stood scowling, holding the wrought iron door knob in her hand.

'You said you were gonna get this fixed.'

Raven tossed the knob onto the oak console table, knocking over a rack of leaflets entitled: A Fabulous Festive Season at Snowflake Inn. Evie and her mum had spent days using various design and photo editing software to produce those leaflets. Now they drifted to the floor or fluttered around the reception area like colourful autumn leaves. Raven ignored the sprawl of paper, grabbed the edge of the door and slammed it shut. 'This place should be knocked down. Why do we have to do this now? It's almost dark.'

Evie forced a smile, ignoring the fact that Raven had been able to open and close the front door without much effort, in spite of the creaking hinges, and the door knob coming off in her hand.

'Because we need to find out if the latest storm did any damage, and as for the lights, we'll need to go into Michaelmas Bay first thing in the morning and get replacement bulbs if any of them don't work. Then we'll have to get the ladders out and climb up and fix them before we can even think of asking Zachary Thorn and his team to pay us an unscheduled visit. We want Snowflake Inn to look its sparkling best, don't we?'

'The only way to do that is to set the place on fire and rebuild it with the insurance money.'

Evie blinked at her niece. That might actually solve their problems. If only it were that simple.

'No matter how bad things become none of us could ever do that, Raven. Partly because we wouldn't dream of doing anything illegal and partly because, in spite of it looking its age, it would break all our hearts if anything happened to this inn. Snowflake Inn has stood proudly on this little isle for almost four centuries and neither time nor tide has lessened its beauty.'

'Whatever. I'm gonna see what Grandpa is up to. You don't need me to help you count lights. I hate maths, anyway.' Raven turned away and stomped through the puddles sending arcs of water into the air in front of her as she followed in the direction of her grandfather, heading to the east end of the sixteenth-century building.

Raven was right about the door knob. Evie had said she'd get it fixed, although it only seemed to come off in Raven's hands. Evie had told her dad about it and he'd smiled and said he'd add it to his list. She should probably add it to her own list. She kept hers on her phone; he seemed to keep his in his head and from the sheer number of things still outstanding, his list must be erased every night when he went to sleep. She'd asked him to fix the hinges weeks ago.

'At least it's not raining,' Evie yelled, before Raven disappeared around the side of the inn. 'That's one good thing.'

'For about five seconds,' came a stroppy reply.

In complete contrast to Evie's dad, her niece could find something bad in everything – even when things were going well. According to Raven, the Starrs were doomed. And not just the Starr family. Raven didn't think the future looked bright for anyone. She was going through what Raven's mother – Evie's sister, Severine – called, 'Raven's dark phase'. Which was probably why Severine had buggered off to New York for two weeks and left Raven at Snowflake Inn.

'Raven hates New York,' Severine had said, when she phoned to inform them of Raven's impending visit. 'She insisted I visit Harvey's family without her. You know how she is with strangers. She told me she wanted to spend some quality time with her wonderful aunt and fabulous grandparents.'

Severine had clearly made most of that up, because by the end of the day Raven arrived, she asked: 'When can I leave this hellhole and go home to London? I'm fifteen and perfectly capable of looking after myself.'

'Social services may not agree,' Evie's mother, Molly had replied.

Evie's gran did nothing to improve Raven's mood. 'I came here seventy-three years ago when I was your age and I've never left.'

'Jesus, Grammie! How many more times are you gonna tell me that?' Raven tossed a lock of waist-length black hair over her shoulder and stormed up to her room, slamming the door so hard that the downstairs windows rattled. That was two days ago.

The future for the Starrs wasn't looking very bright – or very merry – unless they found a pot of gold, and Raven's mood altered drastically. That would take a lot more than miracles or magic. But Zachary Thorn might help with that, too, in a roundabout way. If not, it was going to be a pretty grim Christmas this year – and possibly the last Christmas the Starr family would spend at Snowflake Inn.

Chapter Two

Evie peered up at the Christmas lights draped along the full-length of the outside of the inn. They were swaying limply in the wind and looked more like a row of wet socks dangling from a washing line than the 'glowing crystal icicles capturing the iridescent colours of the Aurora Borealis' – which was how they had been described on the box they came in, two or three years ago. For the price they cost, Evie could have paid for a trip to see the real Northern Lights. OK. Slight exaggeration. But they were bloody expensive and they shouldn't look like this after only a couple of years. Several of the bulbs were dead, some were broken and the rest were dim or colourless in the fading, late afternoon light. Hardly the sparkling, colourful and glowing sight Evie was going for. Festive lights should offer warmth and cheer to approaching guests, not look washed out and broken. Guests might get the impression that the inside was equally as cold and unwelcoming. She drew a rough diagram with an app she'd downloaded to her phone and made a note of how many bulbs were dead. At this rate, it would probably be cheaper to buy a brand new set. Her heart sank at the thought.

Raven reappeared, her black coat flapping as if she actually was about to take flight. She didn't weigh much more than a feather by the looks of her. If the wind picked up to the strength it had last night, Raven stood a good chance of being blown away. The poor girl looked miserable with her head bowed and her hands shoved deep into her pockets. Evie's heart went out to her. Severine had no right to go off to New York with her latest boyfriend to meet his family, and leave her daughter behind, especially at this time of year. Severine would return in time for Christmas, possibly with her new man Harvey in tow, but that wasn't the point. Raven needed her mum, as much as she tried to pretend otherwise.

Evie tapped the call button on her phone, pressed it against one ear and cupped her hand against the other, like ill-matched ear muffs. The winds were increasing and the thud of waves echoed around her as the tide came in. It barrelled down the narrow channel just a few metres away between the rocks of Snowflake Isle and the mainland. Sprays of seawater shot high into the air, the spume of which rained down like falling snowflakes.

'This is how Snowflake Cove got its name,' she said, glancing at Raven who was now standing in front of her, sulking. 'Well, because of this snowflake-like spume and because the isle is similar in shape to a snowflake.'

'Thrilling,' Raven said, shoving her hands even deeper into the massive pockets. 'I hope you're telling that to whoever's on the phone, and not to me, because if not, you're getting as bad as Grammie. I've heard that a hundred times and each time is as boring as the last. I couldn't care less how this lump of rock was named. Can I go back inside? It's freezing out here and Grandpa seems to think he's six, not sixty.'

'I thought you'd like something to occupy your time. We could really use your help.'

'What? Standing around staring up at stupid lights, waiting for my fingers to drop off and my toes to get frostbite. Yeah. That's a brilliant idea. I told you before we came out here that you're a nutter doing this now. And you're an even bigger nutter if you think I'm gonna hold a ladder while you climb up and replace light bulbs tomorrow, especially in this weather.'

Raven had a point. The winds were growing in intensity and there may well be a gale on the way, if not another full-blown storm. Plus, the light was fading fast. Perhaps tomorrow would bring better weather. Zachary Thorn and his team would be in

Michaelmas Bay the day after that, so there was very little time.

'You go in and put the kettle on. I'll get Dad. I'm calling Juniper but she's not answering and she hasn't switched on her voicemail. I want to ask if she will look in a couple of shops in town and give us an idea of the cost of new sets of lights. She can tell us when she comes into the bar tonight.'

Raven seemed to brighten a little. 'Juniper Green? Is her brother coming too?'

'Roland? I don't know. He doesn't usually come over. He doesn't live in Snowflake Cove, he lives in Michaelmas Bay.'

Raven tutted and the spark faded from her eyes. 'I know where he lives. I'm not stupid, you know. He's lucky not having to live in this dump. I just thought he might come with her, that's all.'

'Do you like him? Isn't he on Facebook or something? You could invite him over for supper if you want.'

'Don't make it into something it isn't. I haven't seen him since that day we were all together during our summer holiday. He was fun to hang with, that's all. I don't fancy him or anything and we're not all sex-mad, you know. I get enough of that crap with Mum, I don't need it from you too. Jesus. When can I get out of here and go home?' She didn't wait for an answer. She stormed off towards the door, tugged at the edge to open it as the handle was still off, kicked it in frustration and was possibly about to do much worse if the door hadn't been opened from inside.

'Oh, hello darling,' Evie's mum, Molly, said to Raven, who raced past her without a word.

'I think I've upset her again,' Evie said.

'How can you tell? Isn't 'grumpy' her everyday persona? Gosh it's freezing out here. I see the doorknob has come off again. I must get your father to see to that. Are you talking to anyone or just keeping your ear warm? I came to say there are mince pies, hot from the oven and shortbread biscuits aplenty, if you fancy a cup of tea and a bite to eat. I've just put another batch of pies in and once they're done, I'll start thinking about cooking supper. Where's your father?'

Evie giggled. 'I'm calling Juniper but there must be something wrong with her phone because it just keeps ringing and … oh, hold on. It's finally gone to voicemail. Juniper, it's Evie. Call me as soon as you get this message please. I need you to look at Christmas lights.' Evie rang off and shoved the phone in her coat pocket. 'Um … Dad's round the back, I think. Raven said he was acting like a child, so he's probably searching for crabs in the rock pools again instead of checking for damage to the inn.'

'That man and his crabs,' Molly said. 'Oh dear.' She burst out laughing. 'I didn't mean that the way it came out. What I meant was I'll never understand why your father has such a fascination with crabs. It's not as if we can eat the ones we get on the isle. They're far too small. Go and find him will you, sweetheart? I'll put something here to keep the door ajar so don't be long. We don't want this bitter cold to get inside, do we? Jessie will complain we've given her pneumonia, and Raven will use it as an excuse to report us to child services or whatever, and that's all we need before Christmas.'

Evie smiled. Her mum was joking of course, but there might be some truth in that. 'OK. See you in a mo.' Her phone rang and, grabbing it as she leapt over a large puddle, she answered it without looking at the caller display. 'Thanks for calling back. I need you to do me a favour. Can you nip into a couple of shops and look at Christmas lights, please? Ours are going to need replacing. But not the expensive ones. Money is tighter than Miranda Bradley's knicker elastic. Oh! But you'll never guess what. That sex-god, hot bod, Zachary Thorn is coming to Michaelmas Bay. Can you believe it? Gran told us, so it must be true. I'm going to try to think of a way to get him to come to Snowflake Inn for a drink. And anything else he fancies, if you get my drift? If we can get this place on the telly, even for a few minutes, it'd be a gift from the gods. A bit like the man himself. ... Juniper? Juniper, are you there?'

The person on the other end of the call cleared their throat and a deep, sexy and unmistakably masculine voice said, 'Whoever Juniper is, she's not here. Sorry. But who's Miranda Bradley and why is her knicker elastic so tight? I'm asking for purely journalistic reasons, you understand.'

'Eh?' Evie glanced at the screen. That wasn't Juniper's number or the picture of the dancing reindeer that Evie and her best friend Juniper had linked to one another's calls. 'Is this some kind of joke? Who are you and why didn't you tell me straight away that you weren't Juniper?'

'I was waiting for you to take a breath. You took longer than expected.'

'What? Listen, if you're trying to sell me something, forget it. I'm broke. And no, I haven't had an accident so I don't need a specialist firm to make a claim for me. Our windows are ancient, and the building's Grade II listed, so double-glazing's out, and I can't afford life insurance, or any other kind of insurance for that matter. Thanks all the same. How did you get this number, anyway?'

'Jessica Starr texted it to me. I'm not trying to sell you anything. Quite the contrary.'

'Jessica … Gran? My gran gave you my number? Why?'

'So that I could call you if I had any questions – and I have. Where do you live exactly?'

'In Snowflake Inn.'

'But where *is* Snowflake Inn?'

'Oh? Are you planning a visit? Do you want to book a room? We usually don't do that via my personal mobile but if you know my gran, then of course, I'll happily make an exception.'

'I don't know your gran.'

'But …? Sorry. Didn't you just say that Jessica Starr texted you my number?'

'Yes'

'Well she's my gran.'

'So you said. That must be positively lovely for you both. But I don't know her.'

'Then why did she text you my number?'

'I told you. So that I could call you if I had any questions. We seem to be going around in circles. All I want to know – other than the details of Miranda Bradley's knicker elastic – is where the place is and how I get there.'

Evie could tell from the timbre of his voice that he was grinning. She always smiled when taking calls on the business line of the inn. The act of smiling made one's voice sound friendlier. Although this person didn't sound particularly friendly. He sounded rather sarcastic … and bored, as if he had better things to do with his time. Had Raven got someone to call to wind Evie up?

'I know it's close to St Michael's Bay,' he continued. 'But that's about it. A postcode would be good. That'll pinpoint it. It does have a postcode, doesn't it?'

'It's not St Michael's Bay. It's Michaelmas Bay. It's spelt as Michael-m-a-s but it's pronounced Mickle, as in nickel, and mass, as in … *ass* – which you'll definitely know how to spell if this conversation is anything to go by. So it's Snowflake Inn in Snowflake Cove, near

Michaelmas Bay.'

A snort of laughter shot through the phone.

'Snowflake Cove? Seriously? Snowflake Inn in Snowflake Cove. Is that some sort of oxymoron? Snowflakes and salt water don't really seem to go together.'

'And you, no doubt, are the font of all knowledge regarding any form of moron. I think you'll find snowflakes in Alaska, Canada, Iceland, Norway, Sweden. Need I go on? They all have salt water, and snowflakes at certain times of the year.'

'But none of them have a village named after one. It's rather twee. Do you have a Santa's Grotto and a toyshop with employees of limited stature?'

'Yes. And reindeers that fly. Don't be ludicrous. The isle is the shape of a snowflake and when the tide ... Oh never mind. If you're coming to Snowflake Cove you'll see for yourself. Are you coming here, or is this a wind-up?'

'It's not a wind-up. Although I wondered the same thing when Pops told me. I'm coming. If I can find the place. Can you simply text me the postcode, please?'

'Yes, I'll do that. Just as soon as you tell me who you are.'

'Didn't I say? I'm Zachary Thorn. Or sex-god, hot bod, as I believe you and Juniper know me. I'm looking forward to a drink in Snowflake Inn ... and anything else that's on offer. Once I know where the delightful-sounding place can be found. And I'd quite like to meet Miranda Bradley. Any chance of that?'

Chapter Three

John Starr skipped over a large puddle. 'You're looking a bit peaky, sweetheart. We'd better get you inside before you catch your death.'

Evie glanced up at her dad. She had been staring at her phone for the last five minutes. After the humiliation of discovering she was speaking to none other than Zachary Thorn, she immediately ended the call and, a few moments later when he called back, rejected that one. She texted him the postcode, hoping that would satisfy him and apparently it had. Thankfully, he hadn't called a third time. She couldn't speak to him now. There was nothing she could possibly say to minimise her embarrassment. And yet, he had such a sensual, lilting voice, a tiny part of her wanted to hear it again.

'Sorry, Dad. What?'

He smiled. 'Off on your daydreams, as usual? I said I thought you looked a bit peaky, but the colour seems to be coming back. Perhaps a little too much. Your face looks like a beetroot now. Come along. Let's get you in the warm. You might be coming down with something.'

John put an arm around her shoulders and marched her towards the front door.

'I'm fine. Just … a little confused.'

'Oh? What about? The lights?'

'No. Gran didn't say she actually *knew* Zachary Thorn, did she? Or that she'd texted him my number?'

He tilted his head to look her in the eye. 'My mum text Zachary Thorn? I don't think so. She doesn't know him or his number as far as I'm aware, so how could she? Unless she contacted the TV station. That's a possibility, knowing her.'

'I've just had the strangest conversation with a man claiming to be him and he said that Gran had texted him my mobile number and told him to contact me if he had any questions. That's a bit bizarre, isn't it?'

'Completely. Why's the front door open? Don't tell me.' He let out a sigh. 'Raven's pulled the door knob off again. I must add that to my list.'

'I keep adding it to your list, Dad – and to mine – but the list just seems to get longer. We really need to get all this stuff done if we're going to stand a chance of impressing Zachary Thorn. Oh hell. I must speak to Gran about that. It's all very strange.'

She stumbled as her phone rang again; her dad's arm stopped her from falling.

'Are you OK, sweetheart? You seem a bit jumpy.'

Regaining her composure, she smiled and checked the screen, where a dancing reindeer spun around and shook its bottom at her. 'I'm fine. It's Juniper. I'll meet you in the kitchen in a second.'

He kissed her forehead and marched off, humming another combination of cheerful Christmas tunes.

'Oh my God, Juniper! Wait a minute. It is you, isn't it?'

'Of course it's me, you numpty. Didn't my name and the jolly reindeer appear when it rang?'

'Yes but … Oh never mind. You won't believe what's just happened.'

'Tell me.'

Evie told her best friend about the recent phone conversation, almost word for word and Juniper chortled with laughter.

'It's not funny. I wanted to see if I could find some way to get him and his crew to come here, so that we could get some publicity. Even five minutes on his show would boost interest in the inn a million-fold. We'd have people clamouring for rooms. But how can I do that now? Not only did I insult him – because I thought it must be some loony on the phone, or one of Raven's friends she'd asked to call me to wind me up – but

I also called him a sex-god, hot bod. How was I to know it was Zachary Thorn?'

Juniper continued to laugh. 'You weren't. And it might not have been. Just because he said he was, it doesn't mean he was.'

'Wh-at? So you're saying that it still might have been a joke then? It might not have actually been Zachary Thorn.'

'I'm saying that it's odd. I know Jessie gets away with murder, but how – and why – would she have the mobile number of a thirty-six-year-old, ex-SAS officer turned TV star? And if she had, how has she managed to keep it a secret? Your gran never keeps anything secret.'

'She never keeps anyone else's secrets, secret, but I know she's got a few of her own that she's never shared with me, Severine or Mum, and probably not with her own son, either. She's told us a few times that we'll get the shocks of our lives when she joins Grandad on the other side and we finally get to read her diaries. Severine and I searched for them for years, but we never found them. I began to think they didn't exist but I mentioned them to Dad once and he said that she'd kept a diary ever since he could remember.'

'She must hide them well.'

'She does.'

'So … perhaps Zachary's her secret love child or something and she's been keeping an eye on him all these years.'

'Juniper! Apart from the fact that she and

Grandad were madly in love their entire lives, and they got together when she came to live in Snowflake Cove at the age of fifteen, Gran's eighty-eight. That would mean she was around fifty-two when she had Zachary. I think Dad would have noticed his mum was pregnant, don't you? And wondered what happened to his sibling. You've been watching too many soaps.'

'OK. Maybe Zachary's dad was her love child and Zachary is her grandchild. No. You're right. That's too far-fetched even for me to believe.'

'Are you still coming over tonight for a drink? I'll ask Gran now and tell you all about it later. Oh, and I don't suppose you could persuade Roland to come with you, could you? I think Raven fancies him.'

'Raven? Did she say that?'

'Of course she didn't. But she went all starry-eyed when she asked if he'd be coming to the bar with you.'

'Oooooh. I'll see what I can do. I'd better go. You know what Miranda's like if she sees me having a personal conversation during office hours. Should I casually mention that Zachary Thorn was asking about her knicker elastic? See you later.' With a burst of laughter, Juniper rang off.

It was only then that Evie realised she'd forgotten to ask her about the Christmas lights. She'd have to call her back. Or send her a text. But that could wait. What she needed to do right now was find out whether her gran had texted Zachary Thorn. And if she had, how on earth had she got his number and why hadn't she bothered to mention it earlier when she'd told them she had heard he was coming to Michaelmas Bay?'

Chapter Four

The aromas from the kitchen took Evie back to the old spice market of Marrakesh where towers of colourful spices sat like shelves of pointed hats and the air was filled with such a variety of smells her nose twitched as she breathed them in. Three months earlier, her, now ex, boyfriend Nigel took her to Morocco for the weekend as a birthday treat. Having discovered he'd taken another 'girlfriend' to stay at the same riad just a few weeks later, Evie told him she never wanted to see him again, and tipped the contents of the pepper pot over him. It seemed like a good way to make her point. Spices extracted a mixed reaction from her now. But those associated with Christmas – ginger, mace, cinnamon, nutmeg, cloves, myrrh and star anise, still warmed her heart and filled her soul with happiness. She forgot the hurt and humiliation

Nigel's cheating had caused. She even forgot about the embarrassing conversation with Zachary Thorn until she walked into the kitchen and saw the look on her gran's face.

'Before you say a word,' Jessie said, from her armchair beside the Aga the moment Evie entered the kitchen. 'Yes, I do have Zachary Thorn's number and never you mind why or how. You wanted him to come here. He's coming. At least I hope he is. John tells me you had an odd conversation with the boy a few minutes ago. I gave him your number to speed up the process, not for you to put him off visiting.'

'Well, thank you for telling me, Gran. Why didn't you mention that when you told us you'd heard he was going to be in Michaelmas Bay? And who told you he was coming? We've watched his show umpteen times and you've never once said you know him, let alone have his personal phone number.'

'We all have our little secrets. I know the lad's grandpa, that's all you need to know. You said if you could get him here, it would help the inn. While you were off formulating your plans, I got to work to make it happen. You should be thanking me, not hauling me over the coals and interrogating me like someone from the Spanish Inquisition. Now pour me a glass of sherry, there's a dear and tell me about the conversation. Word for word, mind. Don't go leaving anything out.'

'I'll pour the sherry,' John said.

For the second time, Evie repeated her conversation with Zachary. Jessie chuckled. John tutted. Molly giggled and shook her head, repeating the words 'sex-god, hot bod' as she took a tray of mince pies from the oven and placed it to cool on the Christmas tree-shaped trivet on the worktop.

'Sounds to me like the young whippersnapper's got an even better reason for visiting now,' Jessie said before sipping her sherry.

'You must be joking, Gran. I can't face the man after this. You, Mum and Dad will have to talk to him if he does come. And you'll have to show him around.'

'What about me?' Raven asked. Still wearing her coat, she was perched on the edge of her seat and hunched over the kitchen table.

'You're too young to be drinking sherry,' John said.

Raven rolled her eyes. 'I've drunk far stronger stuff than sherry, Grandpa, but you can keep that muck. Yuck. Can't stand it. I meant what about me meeting Zachary? I won't say anything stupid like he's got a 'hot bod', or anything. He's waaaay too old for me to find attractive.'

Molly passed her two mince pies on a plate and smiled. 'That should make him feel wonderful, Raven. We're trying to impress him, not tell him he's past it.'

'Duh-uh. I wouldn't tell him he's old. I'm not stupid, you know. How many calories are there in these?'

'Not enough for you to worry about. Just enjoy them, darling.' Molly sprinkled them with icing sugar. 'That's to make you even sweeter than you are, if that's possible.' She blew her granddaughter a kiss and reached out and stroked her hair.

Raven smiled at her before shoving an entire mince pie into her mouth and grinning at Evie.

'Delightful,' Evie said, grinning back. It made a change to see anything on Raven's face other than a frown.

'Well someone's got to speak to the man,' Jessie said, 'and it won't be me. I do enough around here as it is and he's not going to drag himself from The Grand Hotel in Michaelmas Bay to see an eighty-eight-year-old. Don't I get a mince pie? It is my secret recipe and I did help to make them, after all.'

Molly put two mince pies on a plate and sprinkled them with icing sugar. She glanced at Jessie, grinned and sprinkled more icing sugar over them before passing her the plate and winking at her.

Jessie screwed up her eyes. 'Don't think that was lost on me, Molly Starr because it wasn't.' She smiled and bit into one, closing her eyes and leaning back in her armchair. 'Heaven. Even if I do say so myself.'

Evie grabbed one. The pastry melted in her mouth and the sugary filling oozed onto her tongue as she munched on the chopped nuts, cranberries, glacé cherries, raisins, sultanas and currants. But it wasn't the abundance of fruit and nuts that gave her gran's mince pies a taste that no other mince pies had. It was Jessie Starr's secret recipe and no one was getting that until Jessie Starr was – to use her own words, 'Dead, burned and floating to the heavens over Snowflake Inn.'

'You can do it, sweetheart,' Molly said, smiling encouragingly at Evie. 'You dealt with Nigel without any help. Zachary seems to have a good sense of humour on his show. If he's like that in real life, I'm sure he'll see the funny side of it. And you didn't say anything too embarrassing. Not really. He should've told you who he was from the off, so it's his fault, not yours.'

Evie sipped her sherry. Her mum was right. She was making a drama out of nothing. So what if she'd told him he had a great body. It wasn't as if the guy didn't know that. And he'd no doubt heard it hundreds of times, from hundreds of women. One more wasn't going to make a difference. If he'd got the impression that he was on to a good thing, or that she'd jump into bed with him the minute he batted his long, honey blond lashes, he was in for a surprise. Not that he'd be interested in her anyway.

'You're right. I'm being silly. And it's not as if I even have to persuade him to pay us a visit, now. Thanks to you, Gran, he's going to come here no matter what. At least, that's the way it sounded. It'll be fine. All we want is five minutes of his time and a shot or two of him outside the inn, and possibly drinking a glass of something, stretched out in a chair beside one of the fires. And maybe just a line or two about how picturesque Snowflake Cove is and what a warm welcome visitors receive at Snowflake Inn. That's not much to ask … is it? But millions of people will see our little corner of the world and surely some of them will want to visit the inn? Even if it's just to sit in the chair Zachary Thorn occupied for five minutes during one of his shows. I'm convinced it'll drum up some business for us. It has to.'

'He's a TV star,' Raven said. 'Or he thinks he is. Getting five minutes of his time is like getting an audience with the Queen. He'll expect to be paid. Even that Z-list celeb they got to turn on the Christmas lights in Michaelmas Bay got paid, I bet. Don't give me that look. I wasn't interested. Mum showed me the photo you sent when she was trying to convince me that it'd be all festive and fun to come and stay here. Wrong! Anyway. He'll want money or something. No doubt about that.'

Evie's heart sank. Raven was right. Why hadn't that fact occurred to her? He was coming to Michaelmas Bay to do a show. She was hoping to get him to spend five minutes at the inn and give them some free publicity. But why would he do that? Just because he seems like a nice guy? Lots of people must ask him to do this sort of thing. He couldn't possibly accommodate everyone. What had seemed like a good idea earlier now seemed like the dumbest idea she'd ever had.

But he was coming. Her gran had seen to that. All Evie had to do was persuade him to bring his film crew and take a few shots. At the very worst, she could ask for a selfie with him and post it on the website and all the social media pages for the inn. That would be better than nothing. Surely he wouldn't expect to be paid for that?

'Gran? How did you get him to agree to visit us? Is he expecting money? Because we don't have any.'

Jessie smiled and tapped the side of her nose. 'Never you mind. That's one of my little secrets. He's not expecting anything. Well, not in a financial sense.'

'What *is* he expecting?'

'A warm welcome, a good meal and a drink.'

Evie studied her gran's smiling face.

Perhaps she'd make sure there was a pepper pot nearby when Zachary came to visit. Just in case.

Chapter Five

'It's freezing out there,' Juniper said, dashing into the bar of Snowflake Inn and making a beeline for one of the floral armchairs in front of the crackling log fire.

'At least it's not raining.' Evie poured a large glass of red wine and walked around the bar towards her friend. 'On your own?'

Juniper shook her head and her shoulder-length auburn curls bounced around her long, slim neck as she removed her coat. She tossed the coat on the back of the armchair and grabbed the glass from Evie, taking two large gulps. 'No.' She wiped a trickle of wine from her chin and licked her finger, smiling. 'Mustn't waste a drop. Roly is helping your dad fix the door knob on the front door. He'll be here in a sec. Where's Raven?'

'Sulking.'

Juniper raised a perfectly shaped brow. 'That goes without saying, but *where* is she sulking? In her room?'

Evie grinned. 'No. Gran has insisted Raven learns how to make mince pies. I almost feel sorry for her.'

'Who? Jessie or Raven? They're both as bad as each other.'

'That's true. What did you say to Roland to get him to come? You didn't tell him Raven fancies him, did you? She'll kill me if she finds out I said that.'

Juniper dropped into the chair and took another two gulps of wine. 'You're kidding. If I told Roly someone fancied him, you wouldn't see him for dust. He's going through that 'too cool for girls' phase. I told him you needed a hand with some Christmas lights. He was on his way here before I'd even finished the sentence. If I didn't know better, I'd think he has a secret crush on you. But I think he just likes doing things with his hands. Take that smirk off your face. That's my baby brother you're getting smutty about.'

'What? I'm not getting smutty. Can't a person grin without being accused of having dirty thoughts?'

'It depends on the grin ... and the person.'

'Oh come on. I may look desperate but I'm really not into seventeen-year-old boys. Even if they are incredibly good-looking. And take after their older sister in that department.'

Juniper smiled. 'Flatterer. How do you plan to get Roly and Raven together?'

'I hadn't. I don't want to get involved in case it blows up in my face. I just thought if she was here and he came over.' Evie shrugged. 'If it's meant to be, it'll be.'

'How philosophical of you. Why don't you get Raven to make Roly and your dad some coffee? They'll need it to stop themselves from freezing to death with that door open.'

'That's a good idea. I'll go and tell her.'

'Any chance of a mince pie?' Juniper yelled as Evie dashed towards the kitchen.

A few seconds later, Evie returned with a plate of mince pies and shortbread. 'Let the games begin. Raven's turned the colour of a holly berry, but I've never seen her move so fast. Kettle's on, Christmas mugs are out and she was checking her reflection in the window pane when I left. Not a terribly good mirror. She'll be wondering why she's got criss-crosses all over her face.'

'Huh?'

Evie nodded towards the row of windows to Juniper's right. 'Leaded-light windows. Those little triangles and the antiquated glass distort the view of anything.' She walked back to the bar and poured herself a glass of wine plus another for Juniper. 'Where's Darren tonight?'

'Your guess is as good as mine.'

Evie glanced at her. From the tone of her voice, something was troubling her. For once, it might be a good thing that the bar was empty save for Evie and her friend. 'Oh? Is everything OK between you and Darren?'

Juniper stared into the fire and, as Evie strolled back towards her, brushed a lock of hair from her face and let out a long, sad sigh. Logs crackled in the hearth, broke into clumps and sent sparks flying into the air.

'I think he may be 'doing a Nigel on me',' Juniper said.

Evie dropped onto the chair beside her. 'You're joking? You think he's cheating on you? That he's seeing someone else? Why? He only asked you to move in with him a few months ago. Why would he do that if he wasn't madly in love with you?'

Juniper fiddled with her wine glass. 'Why do men do anything? Why did Nigel take you all the way to Morocco and then a few weeks later, take someone else to the exact same place?'

'Oh come on. You can't compare Nigel with Darren. Nigel was a dick. Darren's … the complete opposite. I was only with Nigel for a year. You and Darren have been together forever.'

'Perhaps that's the problem. Perhaps he's tired of me. Perhaps he regrets asking me to come and live with him in his cottage here. Perhaps he preferred it when I lived at home in Michaelmas Bay.'

'Perhaps you're imagining things.' Evie pulled a face. 'What makes you think there's a problem?'

Juniper sighed dramatically. 'He's … different

43

lately. I can't explain it. Every so often I catch him looking at me and it's as if he's wondering who I am. I know that sounds weird but a couple of times I've caught him really staring at me. You know. Really intently. Like your dad stares at something when he's trying to figure out how it works or how to get it to do what he wants it to.'

'Does Darren want you to do something? Have you had any rows or disagreements since you moved in?'

Juniper's curls swung to and fro. 'Nah-uh. That's the weird thing. I thought things were going really well. I thought … I thought this was it. That Darren was the one.'

'Darren is "the one". You're seeing problems where none exist. I'm sure of it. Maybe he was looking at you and thinking how happy he is and how much he loves you.'

'He didn't look happy. Every time I caught him, he looked downright scared. I asked him what was wrong a couple of times and each time he immediately said that nothing was wrong. Everything was perfect.'

Evie flicked the back of her hand against the sleeve of Juniper's red Christmas jumper which was sprinkled with little snowmen. Evie wore the same, except in green. They'd bought them for each other last Christmas and laughed that it was a good thing they hadn't bought the same colour as that would be too spooky. Evie often wondered how it was that Juniper felt more like Evie's sister than Severine ever had.

'Well, there you are then. You're imagining things.'

'Am I? Didn't Nigel tell you "everything was perfect" when you spent that weekend in Marrakesh? We both thought he was getting serious about you. Look how that turned out.'

Evie took a deep breath followed by three gulps of wine. 'That's true. That's exactly what he said. But I still don't think you can compare Nigel with Darren. That's like comparing a mince pie with a shortbread biscuit. They're both delicious in their own way but one is filled with lots of delightful things and oozes warmth and pleasure. The other is very tasty but in the end, it's just a biscuit. Darren is the mince pie, in case you're in any doubt and Nigel is shallow and … it doesn't matter. It was a crappy analogy. A shortbread doesn't cheat. A shortbread is just a shortbread.'

That made Juniper smile, but not for long. 'I can't put my finger on it, Evie. I just get the feeling he's hiding something and that worries me. I didn't think Darren and I had any secrets. Now I'm not so sure.'

Raven came charging into the bar like a black rhino. A thin black rhino.

'Well, thank you very much!' she hissed. 'You could've told me I had flour all over my face. And not just a raisin but also a cherry in my hair. Now he thinks I'm a complete halfwit. And who the hell is Carmen Miranda? Grandpa said that's what you'll all call me from now on. I don't care if I'm only fifteen. I want a beer and don't you dare tell me I can't have one.'

Evie held up her hands. 'Hey! … Carmen.' She couldn't help herself. It was quite funny, after all. Even Juniper was fighting a grin. 'Firstly, you didn't have anything in your hair or on your face when I left the kitchen, so don't shout at me. You must have done that afterwards. Carmen Miranda is – or was – a singer, I think. Or a dancer. Or both. Anyway, she was famous for wearing fruit on her head. Or hats covered in fruit, or something. And if you want a beer, have a beer. But only a half. Not a pint. What did Roland say then?'

Raven glowered at her. 'Nothing. He just looked at me like he wasn't sure what the hell I was. Then Grandpa took the cherry out of my hair and ate it. Actually ate it! He's disgusting. I wanted the ground to open up and swallow me.'

'But instead you came charging in here. Don't you think you could have … oh I don't know … laughed it off or something?'

Raven's eyes were like pools of burning tar. 'Laugh it off? Are you mad? There is nothing funny about having fruit in your hair, flour on your face and being part of a family of lunatics. Believe me. Nothing funny at all. I'm calling mum and insisting she lets me go home. I've had about as much of this place as I can stand.' She grabbed a bottle of lager and ran along the hall to the flight of stairs leading to her room.

'Oh dear,' Juniper said. 'And I think I've got problems.'

'I think we need more wine.'

Evie refilled their glasses and had just returned to her seat when her dad came into the bar, rubbing his hands together. Juniper's brother Roland followed behind, carrying two empty mugs.

'Goodness it's cold out there sweetheart, but with Roland's help I've fixed the doorknob and hopefully the hinges too. I think I've upset Raven again though. I saw her dart in this direction.'

'Raven's gone to her room,' Evie said. 'She wasn't feeling well.'

'Oh? It wasn't because I called her Carmen Miranda, was it?'

'I don't think that helped, Dad.'

'That child is so sensitive. She's just like her mother was at her age. Do you remember, Evie? Severine was always stamping her foot and running to her room. Even in her twenties.' He grinned and shook his head as if they were fond memories.

'How can I forget?' Evie didn't recall them quite so fondly. Severine's little tantrums had usually been Evie's 'fault', although Evie rarely knew what it was she was supposed to have done to cause them. For the most part, Evie and the rest of the family just put up with them but when Severine discovered she was pregnant at twenty-one, Evie said, 'That's definitely not my fault. You've only got yourself to blame for this one.'

Severine didn't speak to her for weeks. That was a time Evie *did* remember fondly. Evie did love her sister, and Severine loved her, Evie knew that. They simply didn't *like* each other very much. The only thing they had in common was their family and although Severine was two years older than Evie, she didn't act like it.

'Beer, Roland?' John walked to the bar and poured himself a pint, holding up an empty glass and waving it at Roland.

Roland's head was bent, his jacket collar up, and he was looking directly at Evie beneath his dark lashes. His cheeks flushed and his eyes sparkled as he edged closer. 'Er. Yes please.' His gaze didn't deviate from Evie's face.

Evie shifted in her chair. She'd known Roland since the moment he was born. They got on well whenever she saw him, but he could be so intense at times. More than once it crossed her mind that, given the right circumstances, Roland could turn into a serial killer.

Juniper was auburn and took after her mum in the looks department. Roland had hair almost as black as Raven's and eyes to match. Roland's skin was a shade darker than Juniper's pale olive complexion, and even at seventeen the boy could be a heartbreaker, Evie was certain of that. He also had a smile that, in Evie's opinion, no teenage boy should have. It was positively dangerous. Just like his dad's had been. Roland was the spitting image of his Italian dad – who was a bit of a lothario and returned to Italy soon after Roland's second birthday. At least that was the story. Jessie said she wouldn't have been surprised if Sylvie – Juniper and Roland's mum – had killed the man and buried him in the back garden, possibly because despite fathering two children, he still wouldn't marry her. Sylvie had certainly been quick enough to get over him and marry her neighbour, Peter Green. She even changed her children's surnames. Evie doubted there was any truth in her gran's theory, but one thing was certain: Roggero Tazzeone's whereabouts was a complete mystery.

'Hi Evangeline,' Roland said, perching on the arm of Juniper's chair and staring intently into Evie's eyes. 'Sis said you needed a hand with some lights.'

Evie sat further back in her chair. 'Hi Roland. Um … yes. But not tonight. It's too dark to see what we're doing.'

Roland always used her full name. Several times she'd told him to call her Evie but he said he liked Evangeline. No one except his sister called him Roly. He had been a tubby child and sisters can be cruel, but Roland didn't seem to mind.

'I'm free tomorrow. College has closed for the holidays. Or any day if tomorrow's not cool. I'll give you my number. Text me.' He smiled at her in a way that said a whole lot more than "text me".

Evie's cheeks burned but it had nothing to do with the heat from the blazing log fire. Juniper's throwaway comment might not have been too far off the mark. Did Roland have a secret crush on his sister's best friend?

Oh hell. That was the last thing Evie needed.

Chapter Six

Evie threw open the curtains in Raven's bedroom and screwed up her eyes against the light for a second time this morning. It had been several days, if not weeks, since the sun had shone on Snowflake Cove and it was taking some getting used to. When she had opened her own curtains just before eight a.m. and watched the sun rising on the horizon, she had shielded her eyes, like a vampire exposed to sudden daylight.

Golden rays now flooded Raven's room, painting the whitewashed walls with a pale lemon sheen.

'Rise and shine, sleepyhead,' Evie said, in a singsong tone. 'We're going to buy Christmas trees.'

Pig-like grunts emanated from beneath Raven's duvet.

'What was that, Raven? You'll be downstairs in ten minutes?'

'Go away.'

'That's not very festive.'

'Whatever.'

'Come on. It'll be fun.'

'Leave me alone. It's the middle of the night.'

'It's nine-fifteen. Mum's cooking breakfast. Bacon, eggs, mushrooms, the works.'

'I'm not hungry.'

'Hmmm. That's exactly what Roland said when he arrived five minutes ago, but once he got a whiff of grilled bacon, he seemed to change his mind.'

Raven sat bolt upright, her face contorted as the sunlight hit her in the eyes. 'Jesus! Is that the sun?' She raised a hand in front of her face, just as Evie had done.

Evie laughed. 'Yep. Bit of a shock, I know.'

'Roland's here?'

'Yep. We were discussing Christmas trees last night and he offered to help, so Juniper's lent him her car. We're off to Merry's Christmas Tree Farm and then into town to sort out the lights. He's going to give us a hand with those too, so he'll probably be here all day. Juniper picked him up, drove to her office then he drove here. All we're waiting for now, is you.'

Raven yawned and stretched before tumbling out of bed and padding towards her en-suite shower. 'I'll be as quick as I can. Don't go without me. I hope there's some hot water.'

Evie ruffled Raven's hair as she walked past. 'We won't. Don't worry. And yes. There's plenty of hot water.'

Raven took the en-suite for granted, little knowing that Evie's granddad had gone to great expense to install bathroom facilities to all the guest bedrooms, way back in the early nineteen-fifties after the Town and Country Planning Act of 1947 came in. He had been a man of vision and had realised how popular such things would become, long before many people understood the concept. He also seemed to anticipate how difficult it would be to get permission in the future. Evie's own dad had fought long and hard and at equally great expense to be allowed to update them even a little. If they'd tried to get permission now, they would probably have failed.

Leaving Raven to it, Evie headed back downstairs, smiling. So there was a way to get Raven out of bed before noon. Who knew?

She sauntered into the kitchen and was met by one of Roland's piercing looks. This was going to be an interesting day. Her and two intense teenagers. What could possibly go wrong?

'She'll be down soon,' Evie said, avoiding Roland's stare and sitting at the opposite end of the large kitchen table. 'Are the two guests down yet?'

Molly shook her head, her ginger bob swishing about her florid, freckled face. 'No, but they've got until ten.' She had been standing over a hot stove for about an hour already this morning, baking more mince pies and three batches of sausage rolls. Evie wondered if her mum knew something she didn't. There must be a good reason why they needed so many of both. Evie had dusted and hoovered the dining room, reception area, lounge and bar whilst her mum had baked and the smells of spices and sausage meat had made Evie ravenous.

'So what's the plan,' John asked, pulling out a chair between Roland and Jessie and plonking himself on the seat, a broad smile on his jovial face.

Jessie looked startled. 'Plan? I don't have a plan. What're you talking about?'

John eyed her beneath furrowed brows. 'It wasn't an accusation, Mum. It was a question. And it was directed at Evie, not you.' He slipped an arm around Jessie's shoulder and grinned. 'Why? Are you hiding something from us?'

Jessie shrugged him off. 'Don't be ridiculous. What is this plan of yours then, Evie?'

Evie grinned. 'To deck the halls with boughs of holly. And all that sort of stuff. Roland's got Juniper's car and we're going to select the trees before heading into town. Would you like to come?'

Jessie raised her brows. 'I can't think of anything I'd rather do. Oh wait a minute. Yes, I can. My armchair and the crossword are calling me. You're on your own.' She slathered honey on her buttered toast and hummed along with the Christmas carol playing on the radio.

John joined in and a few seconds later as Molly placed a plate of bacon, eggs, mushrooms and tomatoes in front of Evie, Molly started singing the words to 'Ding Dong Merrily on High'. Evie wasn't going to be left out. She sang at the top of her voice. To her surprise, Roland did the same. His voice was far better than any of theirs, but he had been a soloist in The Holy Redeemer's Church Choir in Michaelmas Bay for many years, so that was to be expected ... until he decided being a choirboy wasn't cool.

'What's going on?' Raven asked, from the kitchen doorway, causing a brief lull in the singsong. 'I thought someone was murdering all of you. Oh! Not you, Roland. You're ace. I mean … Your voice is ace, not you. No! Um.' Her complexion was the colour of the tomatoes on Evie's plate.

'We know what you mean,' Evie said.

Raven threw her a brief, appreciative smile before turning to Molly. 'May I have some breakfast please, Granny M?'

Molly beamed at her. 'Of course, darling. But you have to sing for it.'

Jessie tutted. 'You sing for your supper, not breakfast.'

'I'm not singing for anything, Grammie,' Raven told Jessie.

'Not in this kitchen,' Molly said, still beaming.

Jessie shrugged and resumed the carol seconds before it ended.

Evie smiled and drank her coffee. This was a first. Not only were they all sitting around the kitchen table eating breakfast together, but Raven actually seemed to be in a good mood. Perhaps they should invite Roland over every day during Raven's visit.

She glanced in his direction, meeting an intense gaze from eyes that shone like the jet in her gran's favourite earrings. There was an odd sort of smile on his lips as she quickly looked away.

Perhaps that wasn't such a good idea. Having Raven in a bad mood might be preferable to being the object of desire of a teenager with a crush.

Chapter Seven

Roland turned right from the main road to Michaelmas Bay and Juniper's Nissan Juke bumped and splashed along the muddy track leading to Merry's Christmas Tree Farm.

'I don't know how they get away with calling this place a farm,' Raven said. 'It's just one field.'

Evie leant forward. She had climbed onto the back seat the minute they walked across the bridge and got to the car park, ensuring Juniper would sit beside Roland in the front. It seemed like a good idea at the time, but as Roland had spent the entire journey, or most of it, glancing at Evie via the rear view mirror, it may have been a mistake.

'Now you're getting as bad as Gran. You say that every time you come here.'

Raven was right though. Merry's Christmas Tree Farm was just a field, but it was part of the much larger Merry Farm and was run by Robin Merry, youngest son of Ashley and Ava Merry as a side line, once a year. The Merry family had owned the mainly arable farm for centuries, but farming wasn't what it used to be and Robin, who at seventeen, was currently studying for his A-levels, was considering alternative careers. In the meantime, since he was a young boy, he had sold Christmas trees from one particular field at the entrance to the farm. A makeshift wooden sign was erected each year the moment Merry's Christmas Tree Farm was trading. That was usually the second week of December and it remained open until five p.m. on Christmas Eve.

Instead of her usual caustic reply, Raven merely shrugged. She was obviously trying to impress Roland.

They pulled up to one side of the open gate leading to the field and piled out of the car into ankle-deep mud and to strains of Michael Bublé's Christmas songs floating through the air. The sun was trying its best to dry out the earth but the fields and track were still saturated from weeks of rain. A light haze hovered above the ground as pools of water slowly evaporated.

Evie spotted Robin in the distance and waved to him. He ran towards them, sending droplets of brown sludge into the air which landed on his already muddy jeans.

'Merry Christmas,' he said, beaming from ear to ear, his Santa hat lopsided on a shock of short hair the colour of golden treacle. His complexion resembled the mud beneath his work boots, but as he spent all his free time helping his parents in the fields, that came with the territory.

He was the same age as Roland but where Roland was tall and agile, Robin was slightly shorter and solid muscle. A gazelle against a donkey. Perhaps that was unfair. Robin might be shorter than Roland but he was still taller than Evie. Then again, most people were. Not many people were less than five foot three.

'Merry Christmas, Robin,' Evie said. 'You're looking well.'

'I'm looking muddy,' he replied, 'but thanks. You look good too. At least it's not raining. I can't remember the last time I saw the sun. Here to pick your trees? Hi mate.' He glanced at Roland and they did an odd little fist bump. 'Hello Raven. I haven't seen you for months. Still into black, I notice.'

'How observant of you,' Raven said, backing away from him. 'Still into mud and ridiculous hats, I see.'

Robin grinned as he looked Raven up and down. His wink was met with a scowl.

Evie held down a laugh and turned her attention to the trees. 'We're broke, so we need two of whatever you've got for the cheapest price possible, please. Dad offered to pay in beer, if that's of interest to you.'

Robin shook his head and laughed. 'I know.

Your mum's already agreed a price with mine. I think it involved a free lunch for us and some mince pies and shortbread. Take your pick. There're some good ones near my hut. Fancy a drop of mulled wine? I was just about to make some coffee, so you're welcome to join me.'

Evie couldn't remember whose original idea the mulled wine had been, but Robin had been serving a small glass of it to customers for at least the last five years, although due to his age when this tradition started, his mum, Ava had had to be the one to serve it.

'Thanks. I'd love some,' Evie said.

Raven rolled her eyes. 'Why am I not surprised?'

'Yeah,' Roland said. 'May as well get into the festive spirit.' Evie threw him a look and as if he understood he added, 'but as I'm driving I'll have to give it a miss.'

'Oh. I'll have one then,' Raven piped up, clearly not wanting Roland to consider her a killjoy.

They followed Robin to an old shepherd's hut which he'd done up on the outside to look like an igloo. Michael Bublé grew louder the closer they got.

'Wow,' Evie said when he opened the door to let them in. Obviously, there was no sign of Michael, only a Tablet running through its playlist of Christmas songs. Robin lowered the volume as they stepped inside. 'This looks completely different to the last time I saw it. You've done a brilliant job. Is this where you bring all the girls?'

He may have blushed but it was impossible to tell with his dark complexion. He shot a look at Raven and cast his eyes to the floor for a brief second.

'I wouldn't mind bringing someone here,' Roland said. 'It's pretty romantic, don't you think, Evangeline?'

Evie didn't look at him but she saw Raven's eyes light up with hope. The hut did look like the perfect place for a bit of romance. Two sheepskin rugs lay on the dark wood floor and in one corner sat a wood burning stove on which mulled wine simmered in a large cast iron pot. Close by was a wooden bench and a small table and several dumpy cushions were scattered around the floor. There were Christmas-themed curtains at the two side windows and the one in the front door, with smaller cushions to match on the wooden bench.

'It's lovely,' Evie said. 'Don't you think so, Raven.'

'Gorgeous,' Raven replied, staring at Roland.

'No time for girls,' Robin said, with a hint of sadness. 'What with college, the farm and this place, I don't have much time for anything else.'

'You love it though, don't you?' Evie asked.

Robin nodded. 'Yeah. I just wish I could afford to farm full-time, but it's not the good living it once was and Dad and I both think I should keep my options open.'

'You're both very wise. Sometimes I wish I'd carved out a career for myself and not gone directly into helping to run the inn. A separate income would be good about now.'

'It's been a tough year for many people,' Robin said, 'but at least the residents of Snowflake Cove and many of us from Michaelmas Bay always pull together to help one another. I can't imagine living anywhere else.'

'I can't wait to travel the world,' Roland said. 'Think of the excitement, the adventure, the fun.'

'Same here,' Raven added.

That was the first Evie had heard of it. Raven had the chance to go to New York. That was pretty exciting, adventurous and fun, but she chose to stay behind. Being forced to come to Snowflake Cove had been like being sent on a major expedition full of hardship and hazards if Raven's constant complaints were anything to go by. If the girl couldn't cope with a door knob coming off in her hand without having a tantrum, Evie couldn't quite see her travelling the world. But love can overcome all obstacles, so they say. Evie had never been that much in love so she had no idea.

Robin poured Evie and Raven glasses of mulled wine and made coffee for Roland and himself.

'If you pick your trees,' he said, 'rather than come and collect them later, I'll drop them over if you like. I'm delivering one to Jane Dorset in Bridge View Cottage at two, so I won't be going out of my way. I'll help set them up. It'll only take about fifteen minutes.'

'It'll take you longer than that to set up Jane's. She has to have it in precisely the right place. I remember I helped her once. I was there for almost an hour.'

'Ah, but I tell her I'm an expert, so she lets me put the tree wherever I think it should go. Trust me. I'll be out of there by two fifteen at the latest. Hers won't take that long, but I have to stay for a cup of tea and a quick chat, so Mum says.'

Evie laughed. 'That'll definitely take longer than fifteen minutes. But thanks. If you're sure you don't mind. Why don't you tell Jane you're coming over to us and bring her along? Dad will walk her back over the bridge to her house whenever she's ready to leave and Mum will bake another batch of mince pies in exchange for your help. Or you can pop back for a pint or two when you're not driving. Can't take any chances at this time of year. The police are out in force with their breathalysers, even in Snowflake Cove.'

Robin nodded. 'Sounds good.'

'I'll help too,' Roland said.

'So will I,' said Raven.

At this rate Evie wouldn't have to do a thing. Perhaps a teenager with a crush wasn't such a bad thing after all. It had all sorts of positive knock-on effects.

Chapter Eight

Evie, Roland and Raven returned from their shopping trip in Michaelmas Bay just as Robin pulled up outside Jane Dorset's bijou home; a typical two up, two down at the eastern end of a row of four, former fishermen's cottages opposite the bridge linking Snowflake Cove to Snowflake Isle.

Jane, who like Evie's gran was in her late eighties, was waiting in the open doorway of Bridge View Cottage, with a thick, red woollen shawl wrapped around her shoulders. She waved at Evie as they passed. Evie waved back and glanced at her watch. Two p.m. on the dot. Jane was a stickler for time keeping and she liked everything to be precise and in its right place.

'Let's see how long Robin's there for,' Evie said, as Roland drove into the entrance to the small car park a few metres further on.

'I could help him unload your trees,' Roland offered, 'and bring them over. That way we wouldn't have to wait for Robin.'

'I don't mind waiting and besides, there're lots of other things we can be getting on with. Didn't Dad say he'd like you to give him a hand with the roof if we got back while it was still light?'

Roland switched off the ignition and they all got out of the car. 'Yes. But I can do that too. It'll only take a few minutes to get the trees.'

'Thanks,' Evie said. 'But let's wait for Robin.'

Why Roland was so keen to get the trees from Robin's truck was beyond her. It was almost as if he wanted to be the only one to help. It wasn't a competition.

'If you're going to be on the roof,' Raven said, 'could you give me a hand with the lights, please?'

Had Evie heard correctly? Did Raven say she was going to be replacing the broken and discoloured bulbs? Only yesterday, she wasn't even prepared to hold a ladder for Evie to do that. Now she was planning to clamber up there herself? What was the world coming to?

At least they weren't going to have to replace the entire set of lights. One of the first shops they went into in Michaelmas Bay had replacement bulbs for the current set. As that stretched along the entire façade of the inn, that would save them a fortune and hopefully, make the lights as good as new.

'I don't think you should be climbing a ladder,' Roland said. 'I'll sort out the lights while I'm up there.'

'Thanks, Roland,' Evie said. 'That's one more thing I can tick off my list.'

Raven didn't argue and Evie enjoyed the peace and quiet as well as the sunshine as the three of them strolled across the bridge. After the bitter cold and rain of the last few weeks, it was a delight to feel the warmth of the sun's rays on her skin, although it was cold in the shade and certainly not warm enough to go without a coat. The sea was calm and the waters of Michaelmas Bay were as smooth as glass. The tide was on the turn and it flowed into the channel beneath them, sparkling in the sunshine. Every so often, it lapped at one of the many inlets, sending a little wave into the air as if water nymphs were splashing each other in play. The resulting spume fell like soft snowflakes.

'What a glorious day,' Evie said, disappointed that she couldn't spend the afternoon walking along the sand before it was covered by the incoming tide. She hadn't walked along the beach for weeks and hadn't realised how much she'd missed it. If this good weather held out for a few days, perhaps she would get a chance to do that. After Zachary Thorn had been, and gone, of course.

'It's too nice to be indoors,' Raven said. 'Perhaps I can help Grandpa with something outside – apart from the roof.'

'There's lots to do both inside and out. I'm sure we can find you something.' Without thinking, Evie linked her arm through Raven's. For the first time in years, Raven didn't seem to mind. She even smiled at Evie as they reached the front door. Raven tugged the door handle and it didn't come off in her hands.

Chapter Nine

It was a few minutes after three and there was still no sign of Robin. Evie didn't mind. She knew Jane would keep him talking. Jane Dorset loved to talk. Evie was alone in the reception. Raven was outside, probably being more of a hindrance than a help but at least she was happy. Jessie was having an afternoon nap in her room and Molly had nipped over the bridge to take some mince pies to Winnie and Arthur Beadleshaw, who lived in Water's Edge, one of the two, semi-detached Victorian villas at the far end of the tiny village. Evie had made tea for herself, her dad, Roland and Raven and was just about to take a sip when the landline rang.

'Snowflake Inn, Evie speaking. How may I help you?'

'I want to book some rooms,' a rather prim

voice said.

'*Some* rooms?' Evie liked the sound of that. 'Yes, of course. How many would you like and when are you hoping to stay with us?'

'We'll be with you by tomorrow evening. Possibly late afternoon. It depends on traffic.'

'Tomorrow?'

'Yes. Is that a problem? You've got rooms, haven't you?'

Evie didn't like this woman's tone. She sounded somewhat demanding. She'd no doubt be the type who'd complain about not being able to drive to the door.

'As it happens, we do have one or two rooms vacant due to a cancellation. How many do you require?' There was no way Evie was telling this woman that she could virtually take her pick. Only two of the fifteen guest rooms were taken – and one of those was by Raven.

'Ten.'

'Ten!' Evie coughed uncontrollably.

'Are you choking on something?' The woman sounded more irritated at the delay than concerned for Evie's health.

'Sorry. I had a bit of a tickle in my throat. Um. Ten rooms. From tomorrow night. Until when?'

'Six until Christmas Eve. The other four until the 27th. I've had a quick look at your website and they all seem to be doubles, is that right?'

'Um. Yes. Sorry. Until the 27th. So … you want to stay with us for Christmas?'

'Six of us, yes. Is that a problem?'

'Six? I thought you said four.'

'Four rooms, six people.'

'Oh. I see. Um. The thing is …' Evie hesitated. 'May I ask you to hold for just one second please whilst I check availability?'

'Fine.'

What should she do? The inn usually closed to guests the day before Christmas Eve and reopened the day after Boxing Day. It said that on the website, but if this woman had only taken a quick look perhaps she hadn't seen that. Or perhaps she didn't care. The Starrs liked to spend Christmas together as a family, not running around after guests. With finances the way they were though, could they really afford to turn down this sort of booking? Her dad and Roland were fixing tiles on the roof; her mum hadn't taken her phone to the Beadleshaw's house and her gran was no doubt sound asleep. Evie didn't have time to run outside and ask her dad.

She made a snap decision. If her family disagreed, she'd have to phone the woman back and say there had been a mistake. Better to do that than stall now and risk the woman looking elsewhere for rooms.

'I'm pleased to say it seems we should be able to accommodate you. May I take a name, please? And for such a large booking, it is customary for us to take a non-refundable deposit. I hope that isn't a problem. We accept all major credit and debit cards.'

'Give me a moment.' The woman seemed to be searching amongst some papers judging by the muffled rustling Evie could hear in the background. 'OK. The booking will be in the name of Thorn. It's an Amex card and the number is—'

'Thorn! Did ... did you say Thorn?'

'Yes.'

'As in ... Zachary Thorn?'

'No.'

Evie breathed a sigh of relief.

'Joshua Thorn. But he is Zachary's grandfather. Why?'

Evie broke out in a cold sweat. 'No reason. Um. But I will need to speak to the cardholder to make the booking.'

'I *am* the cardholder. As I would have told you if you hadn't interrupted.'

'Oh. I do apologise.' Evie ground her teeth. 'May I ... may I take the names of the other guests, please?'

'All of them? Now? Can't I email them to you later?'

'Yes. Yes of course. That's fine. But ... may I just ask if ...?' Evie let her voice trail off. She couldn't say it.

'Yes. Zachary Thorn will be one of the six people staying over Christmas, if that's what you want to know. And I somehow suspect it is. Are you going to take this credit card number or not? I'm exceptionally busy today and I don't have time for a fan-girl moment. This has all come out of the blue and I have a million things to do before tomorrow.'

Join the club, Evie was tempted to say. Instead she said, 'I'm not a fan-girl. I'm simply curious because I spoke to Mr Thorn yesterday. Zachary, not Joshua. I understood he was staying at The Grand Hotel in Michaelmas Bay. I hadn't realised he'd still be down this way over the holidays so I'm a little surprised, that's all. I'm ready for the long number on the card, whenever you are.'

The woman reeled off the number.

'And the name on the card?'

'Ms Felicia Porter-Brunsnorth.'

Evie might have guessed it would be a double-barrelled name. She grinned as she asked for the expiry date followed by the security code and, as soon as the booking system – another recent improvement that had cost a fortune to install – accepted it, Evie thanked Ms Porter-Brunsnorth for her custom.

'May I take your telephone number, please, in case we need to contact you?' Evie asked, and typed the number she was given into the system.

'I'm Joshua Thorn's personal assistant. Please ensure all future contact about this booking comes to me. By the way, what's this business about getting across the bridge? Is that a joke? I can imagine some people find that sort of thing oddly quaint, but I'm not one of them and nor is Mr Thorn. I assume I can drive to the door and have my car parked.'

'Sadly not, Ms Porter-Brunsnorth. The bridge is far too narrow and there's no car park on Snowflake Isle. But don't worry. There is a small car park in Snowflake Cove and it's directly opposite the bridge. The horse and carriage will be there waiting for you if you let us know your anticipated time of arrival. We'd appreciate being advised of travel delays though. We only need twenty minutes' notice to be ready.'

'This is ridiculous. I saw the photo on the website and that is a cart, not a carriage. I really can't see Joshua climbing into some old cart. You do know who he is, don't you?'

'Zachary's grandfather. You told me just now.'

Felicia sighed as if she were dealing with a child. 'Joshua Thorn is one of the richest men in the UK. Quite why he wants to stay at your rather odd little establishment I'm not at all sure, but I am sure he will change his mind once he hears of this.'

Evie fumed in silence. How she would love to have said, 'Perhaps you should have read the bloody note about transport properly and checked with him before booking then, you stuck-up cow. It's big enough for anyone to see.' But again, she retained her composure.

'I am sorry to hear that. I hope he doesn't. The carriage is extremely comfortable but we do understand that it isn't to everyone's taste, which is why we make it abundantly clear on the website. It's a pleasant walk, if he'd prefer, but if you do decide to cancel, the deposit is non-refundable, as I believe I did mention. Perhaps you would be kind enough to get back to me if there is a problem.'

Felicia tutted. 'I'll speak to him the moment he's free and send you an email either way. Goodbye.'

She didn't wait for a reply, so Evie blew a long, loud raspberry into the phone before thumping it back into its stand. Now she would have to tell her family that they may or may not have six people staying over the holidays – unless she waited for the email from the delightful Felicia before she broke the news. That would be the best course of action. No point in causing a possible row unless it was a confirmed booking.

Well, this was shaping up to be a merry little Christmas, wasn't it? Especially if Felicia, the harpy with two names, was coming to stay at the inn. She might possibly be worse than Zachary Thorn and his apparently, obscenely rich grandfather who was clearly far too up himself to take a five-minute journey in a carriage.

OK. It was a cart. But it was a very comfortable cart and was far better than walking if it was pouring with rain. And if they did decide to come to stay, it no doubt would be. Evie was almost certain of that.

Chapter Ten

It didn't really surprise Evie that her dad didn't mind at all when she told him that they had a confirmed booking for fifteen people in ten rooms and that six of those people would be staying over Christmas. He was actually exceedingly happy about it. But he could find a bright side to everything.

What did surprise her was that she could tell him about it only ten minutes after her conversation with the harpy Felicia. The stuck-up cow must have spoken to Joshua Thorn right away and it seems the man wasn't averse to taking a five-minute ride in a cart, after all. How Evie would have loved to have heard that conversation.

But there wasn't time to gloat. Fifteen people were coming to stay in Snowflake Inn from tomorrow until the day after Boxing Day and that meant there were one hundred or more things to do. Rooms to clean, beds to be made, food and drink to be bought, meals to be planned. Oh God. Could they get enough turkeys in time? They always purchased their turkey from Ben Smart, a butcher in Michaelmas Bay who stocked local, free range, organic birds. But you had to order in advance and the birds were in such demand, Ben had probably sold out. She'd have to call him straight away. And she'd have to use her credit card to pay.

The trees still hadn't arrived – but she had seen Robin's truck still parked outside Jane's house, so he would get to the inn with the tress, eventually. Her mum and Gran would have to bake more mince pies. They'd have to hire some help for the kitchens and to wait on the guests.

Oh hell. And someone would have to tell Severine. That should go down like a cannon ball hidden in a Christmas pudding. Perhaps they could wait until Severine actually arrived from New York. But what if she had planned to bring Harvey with her for a 'typically English family Christmas'? An inn full of paying guests making, no doubt, constant demands on the Starrs' time and requiring a proper Christmas dinner with all the trimmings, wouldn't leave the family much time to have their own Christmas celebrations.

Crackers! They'd need to get several boxes of Christmas Crackers. And gifts. All establishments that opened over Christmas gave their guests a little gift on Christmas Day. Good grief. What do you buy one of the richest men in the UK and his famous TV presenter, grandson? Snow globes of Snowflake Cove purchased from Della Bell's Little Snowflake Gift Shop would not be quite the type of gift they were used to receiving. And would Della even have fifteen snow globes in stock? The gift shop was a room in her semi-detached house, next door to Winnie and Arthur Beadleshaw's, and was only open in the summer months. Mind you, the weather had been so bad this summer that there hadn't been many tourists in Snowflake Cove. Perhaps Evie's luck would be in and the globes wouldn't have sold out. Or perhaps she could just get six. Did she need to give presents to the guests who would be leaving on Christmas Eve?

Could she really give fifteen people snow globes of Snowflake Cove as a Christmas gift anyway?

Yes. Damn it. She could. She didn't have time to run around the shops in search of the perfect presents. There were so many far more important things to do. Plus, she had to fit time in amongst this busy schedule to have at least one panic attack, if not two.

The first one was starting right about now.

Where were those damn Christmas trees?

She'd have to get Raven to pop into Jane's and hurry things along. Raven could also nip into Della's on the way and buy the snow globes. Then she could go next door to the Beadleshaw's and break the news to Evie's mum.

No. Evie should do that herself. Her dad may be enthusiastic about the booking but it was her mum and her gran who would have to do most of the cooking. Unless they employed a temporary chef for the holidays.

They might be able to afford that for a few days. Evie had doubled the cost of the rooms over the Christmas period and the harpy hadn't so much as queried it. As the inn was usually closed over Christmas, no room rate appeared on the website and rates were always higher over the festive season. Everyone accepted that.

Wasn't Jane Dorset's grandson Logan a chef? He had definitely worked a few hours a week in the fried chicken and kebab shop in Michaelmas Bay when he was young. That counted as a chef in Evie's opinion. He'd changed his career several times over the years, according to Jane's regular bulletins on her grandson's progress through life, and the most recent one had involved something about him returning to his first passion – which was cooking. Whether that was professionally or merely a hobby, Evie couldn't recall, but only the other day, Jane had told them that her daughter-in-law and grandson were coming to spend Christmas with her this year. Jane always spent the festive season at her son's house in Bristol and even after he died of cancer more than fifteen years ago, she continued that tradition and spent Christmas at her daughter-in-law's, so this year was special. From what Evie had heard, Logan was considering moving to Michaelmas Bay and was coming to see what his options were.

OK. Change of plan. Evie would go to Jane's, buy the snow globes on the way and tell her mum on the way back ... once she had organised a chef, got the presents sorted, rescued Robin from being talked to death ... and got those bloody Christmas trees.

Raven could ... Ooh! Raven could make a start on the bedrooms. And if Evie could persuade Roland to give Raven a hand there wouldn't even be a sulky face or a caustic comment.

Panic attack over. Things weren't looking quite so bad. And this booking would go a long way towards solving their financial worries for a while.

Christmas really was a time for miracles and magic and as Evie headed outside she sang, 'God Rest Ye Merry Gentlemen' at the top of her voice.

Chapter Eleven

'I've fixed the tree in the dining room,' Robin said, walking into the kitchen where Evie and her mum were trying to write a shopping list. 'You want the other one in the lounge, right?'

'Actually,' Evie said, glancing up from the three-page list on her Tablet, 'Mum and I have been thinking about that. Is there any chance of you bringing us another couple of trees, please Robin? We can afford to pay you, astonishingly, in actual money. Don't die from shock, will you?'

Robin looked perplexed before returning Evie's smile. 'Yeah, sure. But where do you plan to put them? You've already got one in reception and another in the bar. With the one I've just put in the dining room and the one I'll put in the lounge, I can't see where else a tree can go.'

'The ones in the bar and reception are fake,'

Molly said. 'They look realistic enough but because we'll have so many people staying, we want to make every part of the inn look its best, and only a real tree has that Christmassy smell of pine.'

'So that's an extra two,' Evie said. 'Plus, we think we should have one outside, or possibly two, like we usually do. We were going to give them a miss this year as things were looking bleak, but now. Well. Possibly one big one would do it. We don't want to spend all this money before we've got it, do we?'

Molly nodded. 'That's true. We'll probably need to take out a loan to pay for the turkeys. It's a good thing Ben had a few extra this year but gosh, they are expensive, even taking into account his 'loyal customer discount'. And what this little lot will add up to would probably pay for a new roof.' She cast her eyes over Evie's list and shook her head. 'I'm going to make a pot of tea. Would you like a cup, Robin? Evie, go and wake Jessie, please. How she managed to sleep through all this excitement I'll never know. And it's almost dark. Tell your father to come down off that roof before he falls down. A broken leg is all we need right now.'

'I'll tell him,' Robin said. 'I'll give the tea a miss, thanks. I had enough at Jane's to sink a battleship. Does one of you want to come with me to select the trees? Or do you trust my judgement? I can get them now and bring them straight back because Mum's standing in for me this afternoon.'

'We trust you,' Molly said.

Evie turned as she headed towards the hall and flight of stairs leading to the family bedrooms. 'Absolutely. But why don't you take Raven to give you a hand. I'm sure she'll love that.'

Robin pulled a face. 'Only if I tell her that Roland's coming. I may as well be invisible otherwise.'

So Robin had noticed. Evie wondered if Roland had too. Raven did go all doe-eyed in Roland's presence, so the boy would have to be blind not to.

'What's this?' Molly asked. 'Has Raven got a crush on Roland?'

'Please don't say anything to her, Mum,' Evie pleaded. 'She's been almost human since he appeared yesterday. We don't want things to go back to the way they were when she arrived.'

Molly grinned. 'My lips are sealed. Well, well. Roland and Raven. Who'd have guessed?'

'Ask her anyway,' Evie told Robin.

Molly nodded in agreement. 'And if you tell her that there's no better way to make a person jealous than to appear to like someone else, she may even be nice to you too.'

'And reindeers might fly,' Robin said.

Jessie appeared, making Evie jump. 'Reindeers do fly,' Jessie said, gently shoving Evie aside with her arm. 'If you believe.'

Robin grinned. 'Oh I believe, Mrs Starr.

Especially after a pint in the bar. But some things take more than magic dust to make them happen.'

'Anything worth doing or having takes effort.'

'I was just coming to get you Gran,' Evie said, following Jessie back into the kitchen. 'We've got some exciting news.'

'Well, don't wait until I'm on my deathbed to tell me. Spit it out. And Molly, is there any tea in the pot? My throat's as dry as magic dust.'

'Just making some,' Molly said, switching on the kettle.

'OK Gran. You might want to sit down before I tell you.' Evie took a seat at the table and waited for Jessie to sit.

'I'll go and get those trees,' Robin said, dashing off. 'See you later.'

Jessie took longer than usual to lower her frail-looking body into one of the armchairs near the Aga. 'It's getting chilly now the sun's going down. I need to keep these old bones warm. Go on then. I'm sitting.'

'We've had a large booking today and they're arriving tomorrow.' Evie watched Jessie's expression change from one of interest to one of confusion.

'Already? But this can't be anything to do with the Thorn boy, can it? He hasn't even been here yet.'

Evie glanced at her mum for support. 'Actually, it is. Sort of.'

'Now we don't want you to get upset,' Molly

said, placing several Christmas mugs on the table. 'We know we usually close over Christmas but we need the money. Six people paying what is frankly a King's ransom just so that they can spend Christmas in this gorgeously festive, cosy inn, is too good an opportunity to pass up.'

'Christmas?' Jessie's white brows met at the bridge of her shapely nose. 'You mean the actual day?'

'And Christmas Eve and Boxing Day,' Evie added. 'In fact, they're arriving tomorrow. All fifteen of them.'

'Fifteen?' Jessie didn't sound upset but she did sound surprised. 'I thought you said six.'

Molly made the tea and carried the large red teapot decorated with white snowflakes to the table. 'Six for Christmas. The other nine leave on the morning of Christmas Eve.'

'And they're paying a lot of money to do so?' Jessie asked.

'A lot,' Evie said. 'We've hired a chef to help in the kitchen. Logan Dorset, Jane's grandson.'

'I know who Logan is. I'm not senile. I've known Logan since the boy was in nappies. Does he know he's been hired? Or has Jane agreed to it on his behalf?'

Evie laughed. They all knew that Jane felt it was her place and her God-given right to organise her grandson's life in any way she felt appropriate. Thankfully, Logan was a good-natured young man and from the tales Jane told, he always seemed to either agree to go along with whatever scheme she had concocted, or talk his way out of it without causing any upset. Evie was looking forward to seeing him again. He was roughly the same age as her and when she'd spoken to him on the phone at Jane's, he sounded as charming and friendly as he had the last time she'd seen him many years ago. He and his mum hadn't been to Snowflake Cove since his dad passed away. Prior to that, Logan had spent every summer holiday with his gran, and several Christmas holidays too.

'I spoke to him myself,' Evie said. 'He's looking forward to it.'

Jessie's eyes glistened. 'Is he indeed? Hmmm. He's the same age as you, isn't he, Evie?'

'You know how old he is, Gran. We're also hoping to get some temporary waiting staff and general housekeeping, but we don't want to throw money away, so we'll do as much as we can ourselves. You don't mind then? About having guests here over Christmas?'

'Why should I mind? The more the merrier. Especially if they're paying to be here. Has anyone told Severine?'

Evie and Molly exchanged looks.

'Not yet,' Evie replied. 'We're considering telling her when she arrives.'

'I think even Severine will notice that the place is full of people once she's here. You won't need to tell her.'

'That's precisely what we were thinking,'

Molly said. 'God knows I love both my daughters, equally, but darling Severine can be very hard work sometimes. High maintenance they call it, I believe.'

'Selfish little madam, I call it,' Jessie said. 'But we love her none the less. That tea won't pour itself you know, Molly. Do you expect me to get up and do it? I do enough around here as it is. Oh. And whilst we're on that subject, don't even think of asking me to do extra chores. I'm not scrubbing toilets for anyone, no matter how much they're paying.'

Evie laughed at that image and Molly poured the tea, handing Jessie a mug with a cartoon reindeer on the front.

'Not even for Joshua Thorn?' Evie said. 'One of the richest men in the UK, apparently. Oh! But you know that of course because you said you knew Zachary's grandpa.'

The reindeer – and the mug – flew out of Jessie's hand and crash landed on the floor.

'What did you say?' Her eyes narrowed and her lips shut tight and pressed together.

'Joshua Thorn. He's one of the people coming to stay. I don't know how or why, but I'm fairly certain this booking has something to do with you, Gran.'

'Joshua Thorn is coming here?' Jessie hissed. 'For Christmas? The man himself? Not just his grandson?'

Evie nodded. 'Yes. Joshua and, by the sounds

of it, his entire family. They're the party of six staying for the extra days.'

'Over my dead body.' Jessie rose surprisingly quickly to her feet. 'If that man comes here for Christmas, I'm going to stay with Jane Dorset until he's gone.' She strode out of the room like a woman half her age.

'Gran?' Evie called after her.

'Leave her,' Molly said. 'She'll explain in her own good time and I'm sure it won't be a problem. You know what she's like. I think that's where Severine gets it from. It's certainly not from my side of the family. I'll have a word with your father and see if he can sort it out. Now let's get back to this shopping list. We haven't got much time.'

Out of everyone in the family, her gran was the last person Evie had expected to throw a tantrum. Especially as it seemed to be less about having guests over Christmas and more about one particular man. This business with the Thorns and her gran was getting to be more of a mystery than she had ever anticipated.

Chapter Twelve

Robin returned with the trees – and Raven – at around four-ish. No sooner had they walked through the front door carrying one of them than Evie grabbed Raven by the arm and said, 'You're coming to the shops with me. And before you say a word, Roland's taking us.'

'Oh!' Raven exclaimed, allowing herself to be led away as Robin struggled with the tree.

Evie glanced over her shoulder. 'Sorry, Robin but Dad will give you a hand. Oh. Speak of the devil. Thanks for doing this. See you soon.'

John took Raven's place and as Evie dashed out of the door, she saw Robin shake his head and laugh. He was such a nice boy. Why couldn't Raven fall for him? Not that Roland wasn't nice. But there was a little too much of his biological dad in him. He'd either be a serial killer or an

Italian gigolo; Evie was convinced of that. Even his own sister, Juniper agreed her baby brother had the potential to be one or the other. He was a person with strong passions and, very occasionally, a temper to match. Again, just like his biological father. His adoptive father Peter, was the complete opposite and had helped to keep Roland's temper in check over the years. But there was something about Roland that gave him an air of danger … or excitement, if seen from Raven's perspective.

'Have you told Mum about this?' Raven asked as they walked towards Roland.

'About what? Your crush on Roland?' Evie whispered. 'Of course not.'

Raven stopped in her tracks, her face the colour of mulled wine. 'What?' She looked more terrified than annoyed. 'I … I don't have a crush on … anyone,' she hissed between clenched teeth.

Evie turned back to face her. 'Oh sorry. My mistake. I don't know why I said that. It was just a joke.' Evie hadn't been thinking. She wouldn't have embarrassed Raven for the world. It had just slipped out.

'It wasn't funny.'

'You're right. I'm really sorry. Forget I said it. What did you mean? Oh. I suppose you meant, have I told your mum about Christmas? The answer to that is no. Have you spoken to her?'

Raven visibly relaxed but she didn't take her gaze from Roland as she and Evie continued walking towards him. The sun had set ten minutes or so before and the twilight was fading fast as it did at this time of year. Roland was leaning against the lamp post beside the bridge and beneath the spotlight of the lamp's golden glow, he looked as if he were in a scene from a movie. His black hair gleamed and his olive skin took on an even warmer hue. He was breathtakingly handsome, there was no doubt about that. If Evie had been Raven's age, or even slightly older, she would have fallen for him herself.

'No,' Raven said. 'We've exchanged a few texts but nothing more than the 'I hope you're having fun. Wish you were here,' sort of thing. I did tell her yesterday that Zachary Thorn was supposed to be popping in sometime but I think she thought I was joking, otherwise she would have called right away. I'm kinda thinking you'd rather I don't tell her. Am I right?'

Evie grinned. The awkward moment was gone and Raven hadn't had a tantrum. This was a good sign. 'You're spot on, Raven. We're going to wait until she arrives.'

Raven laughed and the sound tugged at Evie's heart. It was a sound they hadn't heard much of, from Raven and yet she had a beautiful laugh. Melodic, warm and infectious. Evie joined in and Roland began to laugh seconds before they reached him.

'What's so funny?' he asked.

'Life,' Evie replied. 'Just life, Roland. Thanks for taking us shopping. And for everything else you've done today. How will we ever be able to repay you?'

'I'm sure I'll be able to think of a way,' he said, in that sexy young voice. 'Not that you need to repay me. I like helping you, Evangeline. You must know that.'

He fell into step with them and moved as close as he possibly could to Evie. She coughed and made sure she put some distance between them, maintaining it all the way to the car park. Once there, she quickly climbed into the back, despite the evident disappointment on Roland's face.

As he drove out of the car park and past the row of cottages, Evie stared out of the window admiring the festive foliage of the wreaths hanging on the doors and the myriad of twinkling lights around the windows. The length of lights between the lamp posts flickered on, thanks to the automatic timer, throwing rainbows of colour along the road and pavement which had finally dried out, save for a few puddles here and there, after a day of sunshine. The sky was clear and there was no sign of rain. More importantly, there was no sign of snow, in spite of Jessie constantly declaring it was on the way.

Evie hoped for another gloriously sunny day tomorrow. Especially as the Thorn party were arriving. If the harpy Felicia didn't want to go in the cart, at least she could walk across the bridge without getting drenched. Hmmm. Perhaps a brief but heavy shower of rain just as Felicia arrived might not be so bad.

Evie grinned at that prospect and hummed to the Christmassy pop song playing on the radio as Roland stopped the car to let old Mason Riley cross the road. He lived next door to Jane Dorset and he constantly asked Jane if she fancied a toy boy. He was in his early seventies and considered himself a bit of a catch. He was carrying his fishing rod and basket and had probably been out in Michaelmas Bay whiling away a few hours with nothing much to show for it except that contented expression he always wore. He was in a world of his own most of the time but he briefly acknowledged Roland's consideration by giving a friendly wave with one slim hand. He'd been a concert pianist before he retired.

Whilst they waited for Mason to amble across, Raven asked Roland where he planned to spend Christmas Eve but Evie didn't hear his response; she was too busy staring out the window.

Was that Darren? Evie twisted around in her seat to peer out the back as Roland drove away. It was. She'd recognise him anywhere, especially in that dark green mac he always wore. What was he doing home at four in the afternoon on a work day? But more importantly, who was the woman putting on her coat and following him out of his cottage? The cottage he shared with Evie's best friend, Juniper.

Oh my God! Had Juniper been right? Was Darren 'doing a Nigel' on her and seeing someone else behind her back?

Evie stared at them as they walked towards the car park. She hadn't noticed his car was there but then she wouldn't have been looking for it. Darren clearly hadn't spotted them either. They were in Juniper's car so he would have recognised it immediately if he had.

When Roland turned into the road leading to Michaelmas Bay, Evie could no longer see Darren and the woman so she stared at Roland's head as he leant against the seatback in front of her. He hadn't said anything so he obviously hadn't seen what she had. Should she mention it?

Knowing Roland, he'd turn the car around and go and find out who the woman was and what Darren was doing at home with her in the afternoon.

Was that such a bad idea?

Yes. Juniper would hate to be humiliated by her younger brother confronting her boyfriend. Evie had to keep quiet. She could ask Darren herself next time she saw him. Not in a confrontational way. More in a conversational, jokey way. Something along the lines of, 'What were you doing home so early the other day and who was the woman? Anything I need to tell Juniper?' That would put him on notice and if there was something going on, he would surely have the decency to admit it to Juniper. Wouldn't he?

Evie didn't feel quite so cheerful now. Why

were some men such utter bastards?

Although perhaps she shouldn't hang Darren just yet. There may be a perfectly innocent explanation.

Evie spent the entire shopping trip trying to think of one.

She failed. But they did manage to get everything on the shopping list.

She should be grateful for that, at least.

Chapter Thirteen

Evie had to tell someone. Normally, she would share all her secrets and any juicy gossip with her best friend, Juniper. Obviously she couldn't do that. The next best person was her mum, so she waited until all the shopping was packed away and offered to help cook the evening meal.

John was religiously going through the lists – Evie's and his own – to make sure everything was fixed by tomorrow morning and Roland had, almost predictably now, insisted on helping. Molly had invited him to stay for supper in exchange. Raven said that in that case, Robin may as well stay too. Evie wasn't sure whether this was Raven trying to make Roland jealous or whether she was simply including Robin, having spent an hour or so with him this afternoon. Robin phoned his mum to let her know where he was – and shot up another notch in Evie's estimation. Roland sent a text to his, earning him a position a little lower than Robin's in the 'good son' stakes.

Jessie had remained in her room since marching off earlier and copious amounts of tea hadn't coaxed her out. Molly assured Evie that supper would do the trick. Jessie loved her food, so Molly wasn't worried.

Raven and Robin had made a start on decorating the Christmas trees. They began by hanging all the decorations which had been removed from the fake trees, onto the new, real, replacement trees in the bar and the reception. The trees outside would be decorated in the morning when it was light – and hopefully, not raining. The other two trees in the lounge and dining room would be decorated by all the family after supper. The plan was to put on some Christmas music, open the sherry, get the mince pies out and spend a happy hour or so doing something festive together as a family, together with the two guests, if they wanted to join in. It was a foregone conclusion that Roland and Robin would take part. And possibly Juniper, if she popped in later as she'd texted to say she might. She had said that she'd try to get Darren over too, so Evie was in two minds about that. Jane Dorset had said no to Evie's earlier invitation but that she'd 'take a rain check', to which Evie replied: 'You've been watching too many American movies and we've had quite enough rain in Snowflake Cove, thanks very much.'

And these days, where Jane went, Mason wasn't far behind, so he might come and help as well. In fact, it pretty much seemed that everyone in Snowflake Cove would be popping in to help decorate the trees and Evie was looking forward to it, once she'd made sure that everything was still on schedule for tomorrow, and after she'd spoken to her mum about Darren.

'So are you saying that you think Darren is cheating on Juniper?' Molly asked when Evie told her what she'd seen.

'I don't know. Juniper said he's been acting strangely lately and she thinks he's keeping something from her and now today I see this. If he does come tonight I'm going to see if I can have a word with him.'

'I'm not sure that's wise, sweetheart. It's often better not to interfere in other people's love lives. Especially when they're such good friends. You've known them both for most of your life.'

'Yes. But Juniper is my best friend so no matter what, I'd stick with her.'

'What I can't quite understand is why Darren would take this woman to the home he shares with Juniper. He's lived in Snowflake Cove since he was born and that cottage was his parents' home.'

'I don't think people think about such sensitivities when sex is involved, Mum.'

'Oh I didn't mean that. I meant everyone knows him, and they all know Juniper. He'd be a fool to risk being seen with another woman if he didn't have to. They could go to a hotel or something. There are plenty of places in Michaelmas Bay.'

'I see what you mean. Perhaps it's an added thrill. You know, the risk of being found out.'

'I don't think Darren's that type of boy, is he?'

'He's a man, Mum. Men do things we women will never understand.'

'Men say the same about us, sweetheart. I think, if I were you, I'd see if he comes tonight and see how he acts. You could casually mention that you thought you'd seen him but I wouldn't mention the other woman. You don't want to cause a scene tonight and you never know how people will react when they're found out doing something they shouldn't. Just leave it at that and hope if he has anything to feel guilty about, the guilt gets to him and he owns up to Juniper later. Although it couldn't have come at a worse time. Christmas should be a time for love and romance and happiness. Not a time to find out your boyfriend has been cheating and you may very possibly have to move out of the place you've come to call your home.'

'Oh God, Mum! I hadn't even thought of that. Juniper will have to go home to her parents in Michaelmas Bay if he throws her out.'

'Throws her out? If he's been cheating on her then she should leave. There is no excuse for that kind of behaviour, and don't try to convince me otherwise because you never will.'

'Hey Mum. You're preaching to the converted. I'll never let anyone 'do a Nigel' on me again.'

'Nigel?' Jessie said, ambling into the kitchen. 'I thought that boy was history. And don't say one word about what happened earlier because I have no intention of discussing it. I only came down because my stomach thinks my throat has been cut. Is there any chance of a frail old lady being fed a bowl of something hot before she starves to death?'

'We're making supper now,' Molly said, grinning.

'Hmmm. Then let me suggest you do less talking and more cooking. I thought we were decorating the trees tonight. I'm not doing that at midnight. I need my beauty sleep. I think a glass of sherry is in order. Will someone be kind enough to get me one or do I have to do that myself too?'

'I'll get it,' Evie said. 'You sit by the Aga and I'll bring it. Mum? You having one?'

Molly glanced at Jessie. 'A large one please, sweetheart. I think it's going to be a long night.'

Chapter Fourteen

There was hardly room to move. All the residents of Snowflake Cove had popped in to help decorate the Christmas trees, or so it seemed, and it was rapidly turning into a bit of a party atmosphere. People were dancing to Molly and John's old CDs and the dulcet tones of Bing Crosby who was dreaming of a white Christmas whilst Andy Williams was roasting chestnuts. There were several other singers that Raven, Roland and Robin said they'd never heard of. Evie and Juniper had. They were used to these evenings and the same old songs. They were grateful Jessie didn't start singing some of the ones from her era.

Mason Riley arrived, together with Jane Dorset, and he played a few tunes on the antique piano in the bar. It was almost as out of tune as the singing and he said he'd pop over in the morning to give it a bit of a tune up. Evie half expected Jane to slap his face when he offered to give Jane a bit of a tune up too. Jane laughed and said that only the nimblest of fingers could work magic on her, which made Evie and Juniper cringe, and top up their wine glasses to forget the image that conjured up.

Darren arrived a little after nine.

'Why are you so late?' Juniper asked when he came into the bar, his green mac slung over his arm and a worn-out expression on his face.

'It's been one of those days,' he said, kissing her firmly on the lips. 'Things are hectic at work. I didn't leave the office until ten to nine and I came straight here. I'm ravenous, so I'm pleased to see Molly's baked several batches of mince pies, sausage rolls and shortbreads. Right now though I could murder a drink.' He kissed her again and marched towards the bar.

Evie wanted to murder him.

'He works so hard,' Juniper said. 'His new boss is a bit like Miranda – an absolute cow. She keeps him hard at it from the moment he arrives.'

Evie choked on her wine.

'You OK?' Juniper slapped her on the back.

'I'm fine,' Evie lied. 'I didn't know Darren had a new boss. It's a woman, is it? What's she like? Have you met her?'

Juniper shook her head. 'No. I only know what Darren's said about her and that isn't much. He didn't say she was a cow. That was me. Well, she is a cow to keep him at his desk for so long when I want him home with me.'

'When did she start?'

Juniper shrugged. 'I can't recall exactly. About a couple of months ago, I think. Nothing much changed at first but recently she's really been putting on the pressure. Darren says they have a big new client and the agency really needs to impress the company.'

Evie hesitated for a second before jumping in. 'You don't think this new boss has anything to do with Darren's odd behaviour, do you? When did you first notice a difference in him?'

The penny dropped; at least Evie thought it had. Juniper opened her eyes wide and then her mouth but when she turned to face Evie, she was smiling.

'Why didn't I think of that? You're a genius, Evie. Of course that's the problem. Darren's worn out and he feels guilty about having to spend so much time away from me. That's why he's giving me those looks. He's worried he's making me unhappy but there's nothing he can do about it.'

Evie blinked. How had Juniper reached that conclusion?

'Um. That's one possibility. But there are others.'

'Oh? Like what? Like he really is cheating on me and he's lying when he says he spends so much time at work?'

Evie couldn't bear to see the pain in Juniper's

eyes. She needed to think on her feet. 'He could be wondering if he should give up his job and how you'll react to that. He could be finding it hard to cope but feels you'll think he's weak if he tells you that.'

'Oh I see. Yes. But he knows me well enough to know he can tell me anything and I'd love him regardless. Perhaps a few days off over Christmas will give us time to relax and talk about it. I hate to see him look so tired. I'll suggest an early night and see if a cuddle will cheer him up.'

'Yes. And I'll go and get him a drink. Dad's too busy dancing to notice there's a queue forming and as much as Gran likes to resume her roll of barmaid extraordinaire, I can't face the grumbling in the morning about how she was the only one working whilst we were all having fun. Back in a sec.'

'I'll come with you.'

'No! I mean. Could you do me a huge favour and bring some more mince pies in from the kitchen. And those chicken drum sticks are looking a bit lost. I'm sure Mum made more.'

Juniper smiled. 'I'll see what I can find. But get me another drink would you please and give it to Darren?'

'I'll give it to Darren all right,' Evie said, and marched towards the bar where Darren was resting his elbows on the wooden top. He looked as if he needed the support to keep him standing whilst Jessie was busy serving someone else.

'Sorry, Darren. What can I get you?' Evie gave him her brightest smile.

Darren returned it with a wan one. 'A pint of anything, please, Evie. I'm too tired to care.'

'Yes. Juniper was just telling me that you've got a new boss and you're hard at it from morning till night. What's she like?'

He gave her an odd look. 'She's very focused and can't abide slackers. It's the first time I've been under a woman and I'm finding it harder than I thought.'

'Not literally under her, I hope, Darren.' Evie made it sound like a joke but she held his look when she said it. 'It's odd you know, because I could have sworn I saw you this afternoon coming out of your cottage. It was sometime around four, I think. But that couldn't have been you if you were chained to the desk. Could it? And you wouldn't have had a woman with you.' She leant forward as she handed him his beer. 'Would you, Darren? Because if anyone had seen you they might have got the wrong impression entirely.'

He took the pint and stared at her. He didn't flinch or bat an eyelid. 'Would they, Evie? Even if they were sticking their noses in where they shouldn't? Even if they were adding two and two together and making five? Well then, it's a good thing everyone knows how much I love Juniper. And it's a good thing it wasn't me you saw at four this afternoon. Isn't it?'

That wasn't the reaction Evie had expected but

before she could say more, Jessie came and stood beside her.

'You look exhausted, Darren. Your parents would turn in their graves if they saw you looking like that. You need to take things slower, my boy, or you'll be dead before me.'

'Thanks for the advice, Jessie. Helpful as always. Cheers.' He held up his pint and took several gulps before putting it down on the bar and letting out a long sigh. 'Sorry. It's been a shitty day and it just got a whole lot worse. I know you're Juniper's best friend, Evie but I thought you were my friend too.'

'What's this?' Jessie asked, looking from Evie to Darren and back again.

'Nothing Gran,' Evie said. 'We were just having a little disagreement about work.'

'I'll leave you to it then. One of those armchairs is calling me. I haven't made up my mind which one yet but I'm sure a glass of sherry will help me decide. No fighting, you two. This is the festive season. Good will to all men and women.' Jessie wandered off to pour herself a sherry and find a comfortable chair by the fire, no doubt telling someone else to get out of it, if she had to.

'I am your friend. But if I have to choose, it'll be Juniper. You're not going to make me choose, are you, Darren?'

'That depends.'

'On what?'

'On how well you can keep a secret. I think I know you well enough to realise you can't, so all I'll say is this. I love Juniper with all my heart and I'd never do anything to hurt her. In fact, I'll do everything I can to make sure she doesn't get hurt. And I'm not having an affair, which is clearly what you think I'm doing. It would be great if you would believe me, trust me, and let this go.'

Evie stared at him. His eyes didn't flicker for a moment.

'OK Darren. I believe you, trust you and I'll let it go. But I'm telling you now that if you hurt Juniper in any way, you'll live to regret it. And I'll also say this. Juniper already thinks you're having an affair. She told me so only yesterday but it seems she's convinced herself otherwise today. If you love her as much as you say you do, I think you need to prove it.'

Now he did look shocked and he blinked several times in rapid succession. 'She thinks what? Why?'

'Because you've been acting differently lately and giving her odd looks. And you're always at work.'

He closed his eyes, sighed again and shook his head. 'Thanks Evie. I hadn't realised I was doing that. I'll deal with it, I promise. And I don't think you'll hate me, come Christmas.'

'I don't hate you. But I will if you hurt Juniper.'

Chapter Fifteen

The Christmas trees inside the inn looked stunning, even in daylight. Having spent an hour after breakfast, stringing lights and weather-proof baubles with Raven's help, the outdoor trees also created the perfect ambience and the lights now sparkled in the late afternoon sun. By dusk, which was rapidly approaching, they would turn into a kaleidoscope of colour and, as they were on a timer, no one had to remember to switch them on.

Evie was grateful for that. It meant one less thing to think about which was just as well, because today had been somewhat chaotic. After last night's 'tree dressing' turned into a party, virtually everyone in Snowflake Cove was nursing varying degrees of hangovers today. Evie drank more than she had intended, thanks to a mixture of joyful exuberance due to things seemingly taking a turn for the better with regard to the Starr family's finances, and guilt, due to the fact that she was keeping something from her best friend. But as she didn't know exactly what it was she was actually *not* telling Juniper, she couldn't do much about it other than enjoy the evening and hope for the best. And she had definitely enjoyed last night – from what she could remember of it.

How the family had managed to get everything done to have the inn ready for the imminent arrival of their new guests was nothing short of a miracle. Without Roland and Robin's assistance again, it wouldn't have been possible, but by five minutes to four, preparations were complete and the Starrs were sitting down enjoying a pot of tea and leftover 'party' food.

The landline rang at precisely four p.m. and Evie dashed to the reception desk to answer it.

'This is Felicia Porter-Brunsnorth. We'll be arriving at the car park in ten minutes, according to the Sat Nav. I assume someone will be there to meet us.'

Despite having clearly told the harpy with two names that they needed twenty minutes' notice to have the carriage ready, Evie smiled and hoped the panic in her voice was not apparent.

'The carriage will be waiting, Ms Porter-Brunsnorth. We are so looking forward to meeting you all. Have a safe remainder of your journey. We'll see you very soon.' Evie rang off and raced back to the kitchen yelling at the top of her lungs.

'Dad! You've got eight minutes to get the horse and cart over to the car park. They'll be arriving in ten and I'll be damned if we're going to give that cow something to complain about the moment she arrives.'

She had never seen her dad, or the rest of the family, move so fast. It was as if the Starrs had been given military orders and were determined to complete their mission without questions or complaints. John shot outside like a bullet from a gun; Molly put a batch of mince pies in the oven, set out fifteen cups, saucers and tea plates, switched the kettle on and put a pan of mulled wine on the hob to simmer, all in a matter of minutes. Raven rushed around, switching on table lamps and the lights on the various indoor trees, plumping cushions, tidying the small piles of magazines on various side tables and the leaflets in the display rack in the hall. Jessie flew to her room and returned a few minutes later in what looked like a brand new and clearly expensive, dress. It was simply cut, purple and gave her a rather regal air.

Evie checked her 'final list' to be certain she hadn't forgotten anything, followed by her make-up to ensure she hadn't smudged her mascara or got 'warm spice' lipstick on her teeth. She then nipped outside to see if her dad had made it to the car park in time. She couldn't see him or the cart so that must mean he was either still getting it ready or was in the car park, out of her line of sight.

From the corner of her eye, she saw three, sleek black limousines pass the cottages directly opposite the isle, followed by a large, gleaming white van with the words, 'Thorn On Your Side' painted on it. That was tailed by a blue Porsche which in turn was followed by a charcoal-grey Jaguar. The rows of Christmas lights strung between the lamp posts cast colourful reflections on the pristine bonnets and roofs, as if flowers of welcome were being thrown at the parade of vehicles.

'How the hell are they all going to fit in the tiny car park?' Evie asked, as Raven came and stood, shivering, beside her.

The sun had set some time ago and there was a definite chill in the air. The darkening, cloudless sky slowly filled with stars as if the universe was randomly switching on its own display of twinkling Christmas lights, but a clear sky meant a cold night at this time of year.

'Wow!' Raven said. 'That's pretty impressive. The old man'll be in one of the limos but which one will Zachary be in, d'you think? The Porsche or the Jag?'

'My money is on the van.' Evie grinned at her niece. 'You need a coat if you're going to stand out here.'

'I'm not.' Raven wrapped her red cardigan over her white blouse and the Christmas-themed waistcoat. 'I'm gonna be helping Granny M in the kitchen.'

It was good to see Raven in colours other than black but Evie had been astonished when her niece agreed to wear the makeshift uniform.

Last night, Evie had suggested that everyone working at the inn should dress in similar apparel so that guests could tell immediately who was 'staff' and who wasn't. The Starrs each owned several Christmas waistcoats. It was a family tradition that they wore them every year and Evie, her mum and Gran hand-made new ones in October, once the nights started drawing in. The waistcoats were perfect and there were several to go around, so that worked really well. Everyone owned dark-coloured trousers or skirts, depending on gender, so those, paired with white shirts or blouses and topped by either a red or green cardigan, made the perfect Snowflake Inn livery.

Evie wore a dark green skirt and matching cardigan, white button-through blouse and a red waistcoat covered in green and silver baubles, all of which were made from different types of material and some of which sparkled or glistened like the real baubles on the Christmas trees. Her camel-coloured winter coat hid most of it, but it was too cold to be outside without it.

'Tell Mum they should be here in about fifteen minutes but they may all want to go and settle into their rooms before coming down to hot drinks and mince pies. I'll ask them when they get here and let her know.'

'Are you gonna wait out here and greet them? It's freezing. Why can't you meet them inside? We don't want them to think they're something special, do we? This guy may be rich but he's not the bloody Queen.'

'That's a good point.' Raven was full of surprises lately. 'I should be at the reception desk waiting to book them in and hand over the keys.'

'Yep. Roland went to help Grandpa with the luggage. He's taken the extra pull-along cart as there are so many people and Granny M says rich people always have loads of luggage. She made him wear a Santa hat like the one Grandpa is wearing.'

Evie grinned. 'I bet he loved that.'

The Starrs had asked Roland and Robin if they would be prepared to be temporary staff for a few hours a day in exchange for an hourly rate. Robin could only do evenings after closing the Merry's Christmas Tree Farm each night, but he happily agreed and so did Roland. Teenagers could always do with extra money, and thanks to this booking, the Starrs would have money.

Plus, if Zachary Thorn agreed to Evie's original plan of a five-minute scene featuring the inn in his TV show, or a few photos or something for the website and Snowflake Inn's social media pages, the bank account might stand a chance of staying in the black rather than dropping into the red faster than Father Christmas down a chimney, as it had been doing until now.

Raven shrugged. 'He didn't seem to mind. Robin's gonna be wearing one too. Granny M seems to think the men should wear them but we don't have to.'

Evie pushed back a wayward lock of ginger hair from her face. 'Thank heavens for that.' She wrapped her arm around Raven's shoulder as the stream of vehicles disappeared from view.

'Let's get out of this cold? I could do with a glass of sherry to calm my nerves but no doubt the harpy with two names would smell alcohol on my breath and assume I'm a wino.'

Raven grinned. 'She wouldn't be too far from the truth. I can't wait to see if she looks as stuck up as she sounds. I bet she wears designer suits and matching designer glasses and has perfect, blonde hair held back by one of those Alice band things.'

'And she carries her Tablet with her everywhere making constant notes and issuing instructions.'

'Following her boss wherever he goes and telling everyone that he's one of the richest men in the UK.'

'And that he doesn't like this or that, or anything much at all.' Evie shook her head. 'Seriously though, I hope they enjoy their stay. Think what it could do for us if they do. Whereas I dread to think what it'll do to us if they hate it here. With all that money, they must be used to the height of luxury. Our rooms are comfortable but they're hardly comparable to The Grand Hotel in

Michaelmas Bay. Zachary and his team must have cancelled their booking at The Grand to come here. It really will be a miracle if one of them doesn't complain about something. Our only hope is that they complain off camera, not on it and that Ms Felicia Porter-Brunsnorth doesn't post a scathing review on every travel site she can find.'

Chapter Sixteen

Evie expected the new arrivals to form an orderly queue with Ms Felicia Porter-Brunsnorth at the front, who would introduce everyone to Evie one at a time, allowing Evie to allocate whichever room seemed most suitable to that person. Evie would hand over the key and ask Roland or her dad to take the luggage to that room. Joshua Thorn would no doubt be first, as he was technically the person footing the bill and he would of course be given the best room. Each person would take their turn, with the harpy with two names being last, and Evie would allocate her the broom cupboard. Well perhaps not. But it was very tempting.

Things did not quite work out as Evie imagined. Everyone piled into reception in one large huddle and several of them were carrying their own holdalls, slung over their shoulders. The leaflets on the console table were sent flying, picked up by someone and sent flying again, this time being trampled over by four men who had the footfall of stampeding cattle. The Christmas tree wavered in its stand, as if someone had been topping up its pot with brandy instead of water. The front door bashed against the wall at least twice making the newly-oiled hinges creak in protest and Roland, who was almost six foot got lost somewhere in the crowd. Evie could only see the white bobble of his Santa hat and for a second she actually feared for his safety. The cacophony of voices was deafening and as the rabble approached her desk, she wondered whether it would survive the onslaught.

'Excuse me,' she said, her voice raised.

She said it again, a little louder.

She was running out of time.

'Oi! Let's have some quiet.' A male voice boomed out from somewhere in the throng just as Evie was screaming, 'Excuse me!' for a third time, at the top of her lungs. A second or two later, everyone fell silent and formed something resembling the orderly queue Evie had hoped for.

A tall, slim blonde in jeans and a cashmere coat raised perfectly shaped brows over ice blue eyes and looked directly at Evie. 'There's really no need to shout. I'm Felicia Porter-Brunsnorth. Are you the girl I spoke to? I assume our rooms are ready. It was a frightful journey. This place is at the end of the earth. We'd like champagne sent up to our rooms if it's not already there, and tea. Oolong if you have it.' Her gaze darted back and forth. 'But I doubt you do. It'll have to be Earl Grey, I suppose. Well? Is there a problem?'

Evie snapped her mouth shut. Champagne in the rooms? Oolong tea? What planet did this woman live on?

'No problem,' Evie said, giving the harpy with two names, her sweetest smile. 'I'm Evie Starr. It's lovely to meet you in person. There may be a short delay with the champagne but I'll have it with you as soon as possible. In the meantime, please help yourself to a glass of mulled wine. Raven is … oh, there she is … um. Raven has a trayful.'

Raven had backed out of reception the second the rush began but Evie spotted her just inside the dining room doorway and waved her closer.

'Mulled wine?' Felicia's face contorted as if she'd swallowed poison.

'Stop giving Ms Starr a hard time, Felicia.'

Evie now recognised the male voice, not merely from a moment ago but from a previous occasion and even before the crowd parted like the Red Sea, she knew it was Zachary Thorn making his way towards her. She quickly scanned his body from the lustrous, honey blond hair to the tip of the well-worn walking boots and back again. He wore faded jeans, an open, black leather jacket and to her astonishment, a bright red V-neck Christmas sweater with a cartoony, drunken reindeer on the front and a light blue T-shirt underneath. He had a holdall on one shoulder and held another in his hand. His smile was friendly and incredibly sexy and try as she might, once her gaze had settled on his luscious-looking lips, she couldn't tear it away.

'Hi,' he said. 'I'm Zachary.'

She mumbled something in reply but she wasn't quite sure what. To her ears it sounded like: 'Of course you are.' At least she didn't say sex-god, hot bod.

His smile grew wider and he let his holdalls drop to the floor. 'We spoke on the phone. May I call you Evie?'

She almost said, 'You can call me whatever you want,' but instead she said, 'Yes, of course.'

'I apologise for this lot.' He made a fist and pointed his thumb, like a hitch-hiker, at the group behind him. 'Some of them are getting into the festive spirit a little early.' He wrapped an arm around Felicia's shoulders and pulled her briefly to him. 'Felicia here is doing her best to maintain order. She can give the impression that she's difficult and demanding, but really she's a sweetie.'

Felicia smiled adoringly at Zachary but the look she threw Evie consisted of daggers of ice.

'I'm sure.' Evie forced a smile. 'You must all be eager to get to your rooms. Mr Thorn, you're in room number six. Roland will take your bags. Here's the key.'

From the collection of keys she had previously laid out on the raised reception desk, she slid the key to number six towards him. The keys were of the old-fashioned variety and were metal, not plastic cards. Zachary released Felicia and leant forwards, resting strong-looking hands on the desk.

'The name's Zachary. Or Zach if you prefer. I don't mind which but I do mind Mr Thorn. And I can carry my own bags, thanks.' He leant closer. 'Don't worry about the champagne, or sending tea to our rooms. Felicia didn't hear, but your father told us outside that your mother's been baking and there'll be hot mince pies and shortbread in the lounge and also in the bar whenever we're ready. Along with tea, coffee and hot chocolate. That sounds perfect. Can you give us twenty minutes? We'll just dump our stuff and we'll be down.'

'But Zachary ...' Felicia began, but let her voice trail off, as if she knew disagreeing was futile. She glared at Evie. 'I'll take Joshua's key. And we do require someone to carry his bags – and mine – to our rooms. My key please. I hope you've allocated us rooms next door to one another, as instructed.' She held out a silky-smooth hand with immaculately manicured red nails.

'Rooms one and two,' Evie replied, sliding the keys towards Felicia, all the while aware that Zachary hadn't moved.

'Shall I wait for Joshua?' Felicia asked Zachary.

'No need. I'll make sure he's comfortable. You go ahead.'

'My bags?' She glowered at Evie.

'I'll bring your bags,' Zachary said, before Evie had a chance to reply.

'Oh. Thank you, Zachary.' Felicia smiled at him but the smile was gone when she looked back to Evie. 'Where's the lift?'

'There isn't one.'

'No lift?'

Evie shook her head. 'No. It does make that clear on the website but rooms one and two are on this floor, so there aren't any stairs to climb. They're along the hall, on the right. They overlook Michaelmas Bay.'

Felicia still looked horrified. 'I hope Mr and Mrs Thorn also have ground-floor rooms.'

Again Zachary replied before Evie had a chance. 'Mum and Dad can manage a flight of stairs, Felicia.'

'They don't need to,' Evie said. 'I've allocated room three to them. Also on this floor.'

With a haughty flick of her blonde hair, Felicia walked away. The next person in line, a man about the same age as Zachary, stepped forward, holding the glass of mulled wine Raven had given him. She handed one out to everyone waiting. Zachary still hadn't moved, but he had taken a glass of the wine and was sipping it as he stared at Evie.

'Was there something else I can do for you, Mr Thorn? Sorry. Zachary.'

He smiled. 'I can think of several things. But not right now. Am I bothering you?'

Evie tried to control whatever was dancing

around in the vicinity of her stomach by pulling in her tummy muscles and standing up as straight as she could.

'Not in the least. I merely wondered why you were still standing there. I thought you must want something.'

'Oh I do. But it can wait. This wine is delicious. Please give my compliments to whomever made it. I'll get out of the way and go and join Mum, Dad and Pops. They're outside with your father.'

Evie ignored his flippant comment. 'Mum made it. I'll tell her it meets with your approval. I'm sure she'll be thrilled. I do apologise if my father is keeping some of the guests talking in the cold. I'll ask Raven to speak to him.'

'No need. I think they're keeping him, not the other way around. Pops hasn't stopped talking to him since the moment we arrived. Pops is my grandfather. Joshua Thorn.'

'Yes, I had worked that out.' She turned her attention to the guest in front of her. 'May I take your name, please?'

'Brandon Carr,' the man said, smiling at her.

Zachary gave him a friendly slap on the back and Brandon almost spilt his mulled wine. Zachary threw Evie another sexy smile and, as he walked away, the chattering crowd parted to let him through.

'I'm one of Zach's camera crew,' Brandon said. 'And I can walk up a flight of stairs.' He gave her a friendly wink. 'Don't mind, Felicia. She's OK once you get to know her. Not exactly the sweetie Zach says she is, but then he never says a bad word about anyone. She is very efficient though.'

Evie smiled. 'I'm sure she is.'

He knocked back the rest of the mulled wine and put the glass on the tray marked 'Empty glasses'.

'This place is great. Much better than that stuffy Grand Hotel in Michaelmas Bay. But probably not as much to do around here. Not that far to go to get into town though.'

'There's a lot going on in the summer … usually.' This summer had been a wash out, but he didn't need to know that. 'There's still sailing and other water sports in the bay, weather conditions permitting. And fishing. There're some lovely walks, both along the coastal paths and also in the hills and through Michaelmas Great Wood. The night sky here is incredible – if you're into star gazing, but if it's nightlife you're looking for, or shops, then you need to go into Michaelmas Bay.'

'The only star gazing I do is watching Zach through my lens and after a long day of filming all I usually want is to have a couple of beers and go to sleep.'

'Well, you can do both of those here. I hope you enjoy your stay.' She handed him the key. 'Room eight. Take that flight of stairs and turn right at the top. Your room is on the left, this side of the inn, overlooking Snowflake Cove.'

'Thanks, Evie. You know, your photo doesn't do you justice.'

'My photo?'

'On the website. Zach showed it to us.'

'He did what? Why?' Evie glanced towards the door but there was no sign of Zachary now.

Brandon shrugged. 'I suppose because you're going to be in the Christmas show. That's what Zach said when he told us the other day that there'd been a change of plan. Anyway, see you later. I'd better dash. I'm dying for a pee.'

Evie couldn't really ask him to elaborate about the Christmas show after that comment and it took a few seconds to realise that she hadn't told him there were toilets just off reception. She hoped he would make it to his room in time and made a mental note to ask Zachary about the show, at the first opportunity she got.

Had the man read her mind? Was he really going to include Snowflake Inn in the live Christmas Special of 'Thorn On Your Side'?

Christmas really was a time for miracles and magic. She couldn't wait to tell her family.

Chapter Seventeen

'It's the least the man can do,' Jessie said, when Evie dashed into the kitchen to tell her mum and gran about Brandon's comment, once all the guests were checked in.

'What does that mean, Gran? Is there something you're not telling us?'

'Nothing you need to know.'

Evie's dad strolled in, with Roland and Raven close behind, and dropped onto a kitchen chair, leaning his arms on the table, a cheery smile on his face. Roland stood as near to Evie as he could without actually touching her and Raven perched on the arm of Jessie's armchair, slid an arm around Jessie's shoulder and gave her a kiss on her pale forehead.

Evie was as astonished as Jessie.

'What was that for?' Jessie asked, trying to

shrug off Raven's arm, but unable to hide the smile creeping over her thin lips.

'Just felt like it, Grammie,' Raven replied. 'That was fun, wasn't it, Grandpa?'

John nodded. 'It certainly was. What a lovely bunch of people. Zachary is as nice in real life as he is on TV and as for his parents, well, Molly my love...' He glanced at his wife, '... you're going to enjoy chatting to them. And you wouldn't know Joshua was one of the richest men in the UK if he didn't have that Felicia woman telling all and sundry.' He shook his head and laughed. 'She needs to get a bit more festive spirit inside her.'

'She refused the mulled wine,' Raven said.

Evie laughed. 'She looked as if she thought it might kill her. What surprised me the most was that she's got a boyfriend. I assume Pete's her boyfriend. He could just be her personal slave. He was the last guy I checked in before the rest of the Thorn family, and all he said was that his name was Peter Poulter but we could call him Pete, that he was in "Zach's TV crew" and when I said we seemed to be a room short but not to worry because there was another vacant room, he laughed and said, "I'm in with Felicia." I was so shocked I couldn't speak and he had to ask me twice what room she was in.'

'Poor guy,' Raven said.

'Oh I don't know,' Roland said, staring straight at Evie. 'She was pretty hot. Or she would be, with the right man.'

Molly gave him a stern look and waved a wooden spoon at him. 'No fraternising with the guests, young man.' Then she chuckled and added: 'I'll tell your mother.'

Roland shot her a quick look, smiled and looked Evie up and down as if he was taking in every last detail about her.

'No need,' he said. 'I'm not interested in Felicia.'

Evie moved as far away from him as she could without drawing attention to what she was doing. That boy needed to be chained beneath a cold shower. She'd have to do something to make him see that he had about as much chance of hooking up with her as she did of her hooking up with Zachary Thorn. And there was zero chance of that.

'We'd better get a move on,' she said, to no one in particular. 'Zachary said they'd all be down in about twenty minutes and that was some time ago. We need to make sure everything is laid out, ready and waiting for them. Oh! Did you hear about the Christmas Special, Dad? That we're going to be in it or something? Isn't that wonderful?'

He nodded. 'Zach told me briefly. He said we can discuss the details tonight. I told you all that there was no need to worry and that everything would be sorted out by Christmas, didn't I?'

Molly put a mug of tea on the table in front of him and he reached out, pulled her gently onto his lap and kissed her full on the mouth.

'Ew, Grandpa!' Raven said, averting her eyes.

Roland stared at Evie and licked his lips. She must stop looking in his direction. Each time she did, she wanted to drown him. She glanced at Jessie, who was watching the kiss with a wistful look on her face.

'It's Christmas,' John said, when he'd finished, and there was a huge smile on his lips.

Molly, red-faced and blissful-looking, went back to take a tray of mince pies from the oven. 'It certainly is,' she said. 'And I think it's going to be better than any of us expected.'

A knock on the kitchen door had everyone virtually standing to attention and when it opened, seconds later, the relief was almost audible as Logan Dorset walked in, although it took a moment for Evie to recognise him. He'd definitely improved since the last time she'd seen him. The photos in Jane's house paled against the man in the flesh.

Her mum was right. This Christmas was definitely going to be better than expected. A lot, lot better if the smile Logan was giving her was anything to go by.

'Wow, Evie! I hardly recognised you. Hello everyone. Sorry I'm late. The traffic was worse than I'd anticipated and when I got here, there wasn't a space left in the car park. Who do those posh cars belong to? Not the lot staying here, surely?'

'Where're you parked then, Logan?' John

asked, getting to his feet to shake Logan's hand as Molly dashed forwards to give Logan a hug.

'Gran was waiting by the door and waved us down as soon as she saw me and Mum arrive. Then as Mum was getting out, Gran popped to Darren's. She knew the car park was full and had already spoken to him. He came and moved his car and Juniper's virtually up against the wall so there was just enough space for mine.'

'I'll have a word with Zach,' John said, 'and see if they can move their vehicles even closer together. They did the best they could, but we may be able to make a bit more space. Does anyone else have visitors over Christmas?'

'In Snowflake Cove?' Molly queried. 'No. Other than Severine coming to us, of course. But she'll be arriving by train. Which reminds me, I must send her a text and ask if she's coming alone or if she's bringing her new man. Do you know, darling?'

Raven shook her head. 'No. She sent me a text earlier saying she'd call me tonight. Shall I ask her?'

'Yes please. Has anyone told her about our guests yet? Or are we still waiting until she arrives?'

'Waiting,' Evie, John and Jessie all said, in unison.

'Severine's coming home for Christmas?' Logan looked anxious and there was a catch in his voice.

'Severine comes home every Christmas,' Molly replied. 'But she's in New York at the moment visiting her new boyfriend's parents. It sounds fairly serious, but we all know what Severine's like. Oh good gracious, listen to me. Sorry, darling.' She smiled apologetically at Raven, who merely shrugged and smiled back.

'That's OK, Granny M. We do all know what Mum's like.'

Logan shot a look at Raven and his Adam's Apple jumped up and down like a jack in the box. He'd gone surprisingly pale. Was he feeling unwell? Before Evie had a chance to ask, Molly grabbed Raven and pulled her towards Logan.

'Oh goodness, that reminds me,' Molly said. 'Logan, this is Raven, Severine's daughter. She's fifteen. I think you'd just left when we found out that Severine was expecting, because that was the year … Oh I'm so sorry, Logan. I hope I haven't brought up painful memories.'

Logan blinked several times before shaking his head. 'That was the year Dad died. No apology needed. I still miss him but time heals, so they say. Hello, Raven. Your mum and I … and Evie were friends, a long time ago. My gran has mentioned you, of course, but it's good to meet you face to face.'

'Friends!' Molly laughed. 'You were virtually part of the family during the holidays. You shouldn't have stayed away so long, Logan. We all missed you, you know.'

'I've missed all of you.' He dragged his gaze from Raven, to Evie then back again. 'I … I don't know if Gran's mentioned it, but I'm considering moving to Michaelmas Bay. For good. Nothing's certain, but … I think it's very likely.'

Evie watched him for a few moments. There was something weird about the way he had just looked at her and there was definitely something strange about the way he was looking at Raven. What was that about? Surely he wasn't the sort of man who liked teenage girls? Not Logan Dorset. He was such a nice boy when they'd all … wait a minute. Hadn't Severine had a bit of a thing for Logan? Evie had teased her about it because Severine was a couple of years older than him. He was eighteen or nineteen to Severine's twenty-one and Evie …

Oh my God! Logan! No. That was ridiculous. He couldn't be … could he? There was no way. Evie looked from him to Raven and back again, several times. There wasn't even the slightest resemblance. Or was there?

No one in the Starr family knew, other than Severine of course, the identity of Raven's biological father. When Severine discovered she was pregnant, she had flatly refused to say by whom. All she would say was that it was some guy she had met at the annual Michaelmas Bay Summer Fayre. She wouldn't even give his name and when any of them asked, she glowered at them, had one of her tantrums and stormed off to her room, saying that they were worse than the CIA. Evie pointed out that she couldn't possibly know what the CIA were like, but that didn't seem to help. Shortly after Raven was born, Severine ran off to London. But at least she took Raven with her. And she didn't exactly run off. She found herself a job as a nurse in one of the big, London hospitals and moved into a house with another single mum she'd met on some flat-sharing site. She'd stuck to the Summer Fayre story ever since. Even Raven had no idea who her birth father was. It was a secret which only Severine – and possibly Raven's dad, knew. Assuming Severine had told her child's father.

Evie glanced at each of her family members in turn. They were all chatting and laughing and carrying on as if nothing had changed. Asking Logan questions and showing him where everything was. Was she the only one who had seen Logan's initial reaction to Raven? The only one who was putting two and two together and coming up with Logan Dorset.

As if he knew what she was thinking, Logan glanced in her direction and as she met his eyes, his expression said it all.

Either Logan Dorset was Raven's father. Or he damn well knew who was.

Chapter Eighteen

It sounded like a herd of reindeer galloping down the stairs but it was merely some of the new guests eager to make their way to the lounge for some much-needed refreshments. John and Roland had set up a couple of trestle tables earlier in the day and Molly had covered them with white table cloths. Evie and Raven had a lot of fun, listening to Christmas songs on the radio whilst setting up various picturesque 'scenes' on the tables. They used ceramic Christmas ornaments including polar bears, snowmen, reindeers, elves and miniature snow-covered houses before adding little plastic people. They sprinkled the whole thing with glitter and used fine, bleached sheep's wool to look like piles of snow. Fairy lights with tiny bulbs were entwined throughout and they, together with two table lamps, the Christmas tree lights, and the glow from the blazing log fire, roaring in the hearth, were the only illumination. The room was warm, cosy and welcoming, even if the table decorations were a little 'tacky'. They added to the ambience and made it seem all the more magical – and fun.

On the tables were plates piled high with mince pies, warm from the oven, shortbread, and gingerbread reindeers. The reindeers were Evie's speciality. She had seen them on a Christmas baking show and had made some right away. Today she had shown Raven how to make them. She turned freshly baked gingerbread men upside down so that the arms and legs formed antlers and the head formed a large, reindeer face. Using tubes of coloured icing, she drew huge eyes and a long, shallow 'W' for the mouth. She popped a glacé cherry just above the mouth to make the reindeer's nose. Jessie told them they were behaving like toddlers, before joining in and decorating some herself. The reindeers took pride of place on the tables.

The Starrs didn't want the guests to eat too much a mere few hours before dinner, but in addition to the sweet treats, there were some miniature sausage rolls and cocktail sausages. Guests could choose between tea, coffee and hot chocolate, or if they preferred, another glass or two of mulled wine. The two guests, Tracy and Trevor Bright, who had been staying at the inn for the past week, were invited to partake. It gave them an opportunity to meet their fellow diners before dinner was served at eight p.m. Although, as they were leaving the following day, this was more a case of the Starr family not wanting anyone to feel excluded from this 'happy hour' than everyone getting to know one another.

Evie saw Zachary stroll into the lounge with his parents and his granddad, followed closely by Felicia, who in turn was followed by her boyfriend, Pete. The poor man looked as miserable as the harpy with two names.

Evie wanted to attract Zachary's attention. She knew that Zachary and her dad were going to discuss the TV show later, or so her dad had said, but she still wanted to know why Zachary had shown her photo to his team. It had not been her intention to actually appear on camera, she merely wanted a shot or two of the inn and if Zachary would agree to be in those shots, all the better, so why his team would need to see her photo was slightly troubling. If he did want someone from the inn, on screen, then it should be her mum or her dad.

Ignoring her attempts to catch his eye, either deliberately or because he genuinely hadn't seen her, Zachary headed straight for the gingerbread reindeer. He picked one up and showed it to his family, before passing one to each of them. They were all grinning as they bit into the soft, gooey mixture but the delight as the ginger and spices hit their taste buds, was clear from their expressions – and the fact that each of them took another reindeer. Zachary even took two. Perhaps Evie should have made some more.

She, together with the rest of her family, mingled with the guests, except for Jessie, who was noticeable by her absence. Evie went back to the kitchen to check on her but she was nowhere to be seen. That in itself was a worry. Jessie had already taken her afternoon nap; it was unlike her to miss any sort of get-together with the guests and she had seemed full of the joys of Christmas when Logan arrived. The only thing she had not been happy about was the fact that Joshua Thorn was staying in the inn. Evie had never known Jessie to take a true dislike to anyone. She could often be rude about someone – to the person's face, not just behind their back – but that was simply her way and she didn't mean anything nasty by it. Jessie Starr merely spoke her mind. The fact that she now appeared to be avoiding Joshua Thorn made Evie determined to find out why.

She went upstairs and knocked on her gran's closed door.

'I'm taking a nap.'

Evie grinned. 'You've already taken your nap. I'm coming in so I hope you're decent.'

Jessie was sitting in the armchair in front of her window which overlooked the wide, bowl-like sweep of water in Michaelmas Bay and the marina. Beyond was the town of Michaelmas Bay, the harbour walls and the sea.

'I love this view,' she said, staring out into the

darkness.

'It's virtually pitch-black. You can't see the view. Are you OK, Gran?'

Jessie shot Evie a quick smile. 'I don't need to. It's embedded in my memory. But I'm not simply staring into the dark. Look.' She pointed towards the window pane.

Evie walked over to her and looked out. Little islands of fairy lights, some white, some multi-coloured, bobbed up and down, obviously decorations on the boats in the small marina within the natural harbour. In the town of Michaelmas Bay itself, row upon row of lights twinkled and sparkled; street lamps and lights within the houses and businesses mixed with fairy lights and other Christmas decorations. The moon was fairly new, so the sky above the bay was black, but studded with myriad stars.

'It's beautiful,' Evie said, taking in the scene.

'Only a little better than your table decorations.' Jessie smiled up at her. 'How's it going down there?'

'Why don't you come down and see for yourself?'

'I'm fine where I am, thank you.'

Evie bent down to be eye level and took one of Jessie's spidery-looking hands in hers.

'No you're not, Gran. I don't know why you don't want to see Joshua Thorn but you clearly don't. You can't avoid him forever though. Not unless you plan to stay in your room for the duration of his stay. Do you want to talk about it? Is there anything I can do to help?'

Jessie laid her other hand on top of Evie's and squeezed it. 'No, sweetheart. There's nothing you, or anyone else can do. I know I'll have to face him. I thought I could, tonight. But when it came down to it, I'm just not ready.'

'Ready?'

'To lay the ghosts of the past.'

'You and Joshua have a history? You said the other day that you knew him, and the fact that Zachary is here and going to include the inn in his Christmas Special is due to that. But that Joshua himself is here means a whole lot more, doesn't it? How well did you know him in the past? Does this … does this have anything to do with Grandad?'

Jessie narrowed her eyes. 'It has everything to do with him.'

Evie waited but her gran fell silent and resumed her study of the view.

'Gran? Did you … did you and Joshua … have a fling or something after you were married to Grandad?'

Jessie slowly turned her gaze on Evie and their eyes locked. 'No.'

'Then … when you were engaged, or dating Grandad? I know you came here when you were fifteen, and never left, so nothing much could have happened between you and Joshua before then. Or could it? Did it?'

Jessie reached out and brushed Evie's hair with

her hand. 'No. I have never had a fling – or anything else – with Joshua Thorn.'

Evie didn't understand and said so. 'But something must have happened, Gran. Were you just good friends? And if so, why do you apparently hate him so much now? And if you do hate him, why did you get his grandson to come here? And how did you do that?'

'You're just full of questions, aren't you?'

'Yes. And I would like some answers. I've never known you to behave like this. The man must have done something to you, or meant something to you, for him to have such an effect on you. Please won't you tell me?'

Jessie shook her head. 'No. Not before I've stood face to face with the man and looked him in the eye. And I'm not doing that this evening. So stop asking questions. Go back downstairs and have some fun. I'm fine. Don't worry about me. I'm sitting here remembering the wonderful life I had with your grandad. That's more than enough to make me happy. Now go. Please, sweetheart.'

Evie kissed Jessie on the cheek and stood upright. 'Are you coming down for dinner?'

'We'll see.'

'I'll pop back later then and check.'

Jessie didn't answer. It was as if she were in a different world. Or perhaps a different time.

Evie left the room and closed the door behind her. She was dying to know what had happened between her gran and Joshua Thorn, but Jessie

Starr was famously stubborn. If she didn't want you to know something, you wouldn't. And yet she loved to gossip. She was always the first to know what was going on in Snowflake Cove and Michaelmas Bay and always eager to tell. But when it came to her own life, she was more guarded, only sharing what she was happy to and keeping hidden what she would rather people didn't find out. Just like Severine. That was obviously where Evie's sister got it from; she took after her gran.

Evie wandered down, via the main hallway and stairs. She tidied the reception and secured several baubles on the tree which were in imminent danger of sliding to the floor and shattering to pieces. Laughter and Christmas songs filled the air and the fire in reception crackled and spit like a backing-singer to a rap artiste.

'It's even better than I'd imagined.' The male voice made her jump.

Evie recognised it immediately and turned to face Zachary who gave her a devastating smile. It literally took her breath away and for a moment, she couldn't speak. Finally, she managed, 'Oh? Why did you need to imagine it? You saw it on the website, didn't you? Apparently you were showing your entire team my photo.'

He seemed slightly taken aback but a second later, the smile returned. 'Brandon's been talking, I see.'

'Brandon? What makes you think he was the

one who told me?'

'Because he's the only one who would.'

'Is it some big secret then?'

He laughed as he walked towards her and the silver bells on the Christmas tree tinkled as if they were joining in.

Evie pulled herself up to her full height of five foot three, but she had to crane her neck to look up at him when he stopped just a foot or two in front of her. Why did he have to come so close? She couldn't back away any further because she would be against the wood-panelled wall if she did.

The fire reflected in his hazel eyes as he looked at her and as her gaze travelled to his mouth, all she could think about was kissing those luscious lips.

'It was.' His voice was soft and sensual. 'But it isn't now.'

'What?'

Her eyes met his and he held her gaze. For the briefest of moments, Evie thought he was actually going to kiss her. He leant forward, his lips parted and the heat in his eyes wasn't simply a reflection from the fire, she was sure of that. But instead of kissing her, he reached out and pulled a piece of shimmering silver 'angel hair' tinsel from her hair. It glistened a rainbow of colours as he dangled it in front of her, twisting it to and fro between agile fingers.

'Isn't it amazing that something so delicate-looking can be so beautiful?'

She let out the breath she had been holding and took the tinsel by the end farthest from his hand, so as not to touch his fingers. They could twist her, she was sure, like they had the tinsel.

She gave a little cough and, keeping her voice as cool as possible said, 'Amazing. Excuse me. I'll put it back on the tree.'

'I could have done that.'

'Yes. You could. But I think you preferred toying with it. I'm sorry but I need you to move. You've rather hemmed me in here.' She glanced to the console table to her right and the chair to her left.

'I think you did that yourself when you backed away from me.'

Her bottom lip dropped. 'I didn't back away from you.'

He nodded. 'You did. I was trained to notice these things. You also flinched when I touched your hair.'

'I … I thought you were going to pull it.'

'Your hair?'

'Yes.'

'Why would I do that … Evie?'

Why did he have to make every syllable sound so damn sexy? And why had he said her name as if he were caressing it?

'I have no idea. Are you going to move? … Please.'

He grinned and stepped aside but a shiver ran up and down Evie's spine as she put the tinsel back in place. With her back turned to him she asked: 'So are you going to tell me why you were showing my photo to everyone?'

'I didn't show it to everyone. Just my team.'

She sighed loud enough so that he would hear. 'OK. Why did you show it to your team? This is like drawing blood from a stone. Why can't you answer a simple question?' She spun on her toes to face him.

He grinned. 'Blood can't be drawn from a stone. And it isn't a simple question. I think it's rather complicated.'

She glowered at him. 'Are you trying to be difficult? Are you deriving some weird form of pleasure from this conversation? I have better things to do than stand here listening to this.'

'I'm not being difficult,' he replied, as she turned to walk away. 'I'm being me.'

She turned back. 'OK, fine. Look. I understand you're thinking of including Snowflake Inn in your Christmas Special. If so, I would like to thank you because that would be a dream come true. But if you're worried that I'm not photogenic – and I know I'm not – you needn't be. I don't want to appear on TV. I just want the inn to. I don't know how any of this came about. One minute Gran was telling us all that your show was coming to Michaelmas Bay, the next, you're all staying at our inn. I know Gran had something to do with that but I don't know what, how or why. I'm merely trying to get my head around exactly what is – and isn't –

going on. Is that too much to ask?'

His brows knit together. 'So … you have no idea why I'm here? Why we're all here?'

'Other than to film your Christmas Special TV show, no. And I thought you were doing that in Michaelmas Bay, not Snowflake Cove.'

'So did I. Pops had other ideas.'

'But how …? Oh good heavens. Does he produce the show or something? At his age?'

Zachary laughed. 'No. My dad produces the show – as of a month or so ago. Pops just owns the TV company. And when I say 'just', I mean that in the sense that he recently bought it.'

'Really? Wow. I can see why the harpy … I mean … why Felicia says he's one of the richest men in the UK. He needs to be to buy a TV station. Did he do that for you? Sorry. That actually isn't any of my business.'

'He did it for himself. A few months ago he heard we were coming to Michaelmas Bay and suddenly decided he'd like to own the company. It cost him a fortune to get it signed and sealed so fast, but he wanted it and he got it.'

'Does he always get what he wants?'

'I thought so. Until very recently. But to pick up on a point you made earlier, you *are* photogenic. Extremely so, in my opinion.'

Evie's face flushed. 'I'm not. My hair is too wild and my face looks as if I've got the measles or something. I suppose my freckles could be hidden by a barrel of make-up but I don't want to see it on TV – ever. But thanks for the compliment.'

'It wasn't a compliment. It's a fact. And why would you want to hide those freckles? You obviously don't see what others see. You're stunning. Your hair and freckles add to your beauty, not detract from it. Oh. And you're apparently the spitting image of your grandma. In her younger days, that is.'

Evie blinked in embarrassment. Had Zachary Thorn really called her beautiful? It was probably a line. He was on TV, after all.

'Wait a minute. How do you know what Gran looked like when she was younger? Does your grandad have a picture of her?'

Zachary nodded. 'Several. But I hadn't seen them until the other day.'

'Do you have any idea how they know one another?'

'Don't you?'

'No. Gran never mentioned your grandad until the day you and I spoke on the phone. Even than all she said was that she knew him. She didn't give his name or say how. Did he tell you?'

Zachary shook his head. 'Not the details. He said he knew your grandpa, William Starr and that they had started a business together "a lifetime ago" – to use his words. William had introduced him to your gran. He showed me a couple of photos of the three of them together and one of her on her own – which he carries in his wallet, so that

144

came as a bit of a surprise. Then he said – and I'm quoting him here – "I've loved that woman since the day I set eyes on her and I have this photo in my wallet to keep her near my heart." It was then that he came up with the idea that we should all come and spend Christmas here instead of at his home, as usual. And then he said it seemed ridiculous to move hotels, so we should all come and stay here for the duration, instead of spending part of it at The Grand Hotel. As I said, when he wants something, he usually gets it.'

'He loves my gran?' Evie couldn't believe her ears. 'But she hates him. Or so she says. Sorry. But I'm quoting her on that. I really want to get to the bottom of this. What else did your grandad say?'

'Nothing much. I asked him if Grandma knew and he said she did, but other than that, all he said was that he'd tell me more about it another time.'

Raven came running into reception. 'Evie! There you are. It's snowing. Look!' She dashed to the front door and yanked it open, allowing a flurry of snowflakes to land on the mat like a pile Christmas cards and a cold blast of air to race along the hall. At least the door knob no longer came off in her hand since it had been fixed.

Evie glanced at the windows. 'I can see it through the glass, Raven. There's no need for us to freeze to death. Close the door.' Flakes the size of one of Jessie Starr's famous mince pies fell in quick succession and were already covering the cobbles.

'But I want to look at it,' Raven said, glancing back at her. 'Oh Evie! It's settling. Isn't this great? We're gonna have a white Christmas!'

Zachary smiled at Evie. 'That's exactly what I've been dreaming of.'

'You, me, Raven, and Bing Crosby,' Evie said, returning the smile as the crooner's voice floated towards them from the lounge.

Her parents had got the Christmas CDs out again, which was a little worrying because the guests hadn't had dinner yet and six p.m. was far too early to start a party. Especially as everyone was still recovering from the one last night.

Chapter Nineteen

Evie's parents controlled themselves and at six-thirty sharp the CDs were turned off and the guests were told that dinner would be served in two hours' time. It was usually at eight but judging by the amount of food that had been consumed during the 'happy hour' no one would be hungry by then. Not that the extra half hour would make a great deal of difference.

The menu was limited – as the harpy with two names was quick to point out – but Snowflake Inn was an inn, not a restaurant or posh hotel. Evie politely suggested that there were several good restaurants in Michaelmas Bay if Felicia would like to try them, but meals at the inn were included in the price during the festive season – whether eaten or not.

Felicia gasped when she saw the wine list.

'*This* is a wine list?'

Evie smiled. 'Yes. I'm sure you'll be able to find at least one wine to your liking.'

'If I were looking for wine vinegar, perhaps. Is there really no champagne?'

Evie maintained her smile in spite of the considerable effort required. 'No. We do have a rather pleasant English sparkling wine from a local vineyard. I can highly recommend that.'

Felicia looked her up and down. 'I'll have a G&T. A large one. And so will Peter. He'll be here shortly. And water. Bottled water. You do have bottled water, don't you?'

'Yes. I'll go and fill a bottle for you right now.'

Zachary, who had come into the dining room with his family a few seconds before, gave a burst of laughter. 'Evie's teasing you, Felicia. There's no need to look so horrified.' He smiled at Evie.

'I think there's every need,' Felicia replied. 'Have you seen this list?' She waved the wine list in the air.

'No. But I'm looking forward to trying the local sparkling wine.'

Evie could almost feel the daggers in her back as she walked away from Felicia's table, but Zachary continued:

'There'll be champagne for you tomorrow. John has very kindly put in an order with a local wine merchant who can deliver it in the morning, along with some other of our favourite wines. We've even managed to get a few bottles of Pop's favourite, so everyone's happy. There'll be plenty to last for the duration of our stay.'

The Thorn party may be happy but Evie wasn't. She shoved open the kitchen door and spotted her dad warming his hands by the kitchen Aga. 'What's this about you ordering champagne and other, no doubt eye-poppingly expensive, wine? There's nothing wrong with our wine list. We've got some very good wines.'

'But not quite what Joshua and his family are used to, sweetheart. Besides it's not a problem. Joshua paid for it all upfront and told me to add twenty-five per cent to the bill. Zachary even said that we can keep any that aren't opened. They've chosen some extremely good labels. I'm looking forward to trying a glass of one or two myself. Everyone's happy. Anthony, from Michaelmas Bay Wines will be getting a fantastic cut, and we've made more on this wine order than we could in a couple of months of being fully booked. It's a miracle in every bottle.'

'Oh I see. Well in that case I suppose it's fine. Is there any sign of Gran? Is she coming down for dinner? I don't know why she won't. It's not as if we're eating with the guests.'

Molly shook her head. 'She texted me from her room to say she's not very hungry but could someone take her up a sherry and some cheese and biscuits. Cheese and biscuits, my eye. Logan here is doing a grand job so she'll have more than cheese and biscuits. I'll pop up and see her as soon

149

as the starters are all out.'

'I'd better go and finish taking orders then. Roland? Are you staying to do the drinks or is Robin coming to take over?'

'Robin's coming. But I'll do them until he gets here.'

'Great. So far we need two large G&Ts and a bottle of water for the harpy with two names. Damn. I forgot to ask if she wanted sparkling or still. I suppose she'll expect me to know. Take her both and let her pick.'

Roland smiled and brushed his arm against hers as he walked past her to the bar. 'You look stressed, Evangeline. I could give you a shoulder massage, or something. That might help. I'm good with my hands.'

'I bet you are.' She moved away and caught Logan looking at her whilst he was stirring the gravy. 'How are you enjoying it so far, Logan?'

'Loving it, thanks. It's good to be back here.'

'I bet you can't wait to see Severine, can you?'

He didn't even flinch. 'No. It'll be interesting to see if she's changed at all. You've changed a lot – in looks, but not in personality.'

'Is that good or bad? Forget it. I'd rather not know. Severine's the same as she always was. No. Actually she's even prettier now. Raven's gorgeous, isn't she? But she doesn't really take after her mum, does she? What do you think?'

He shrugged. 'She's very pretty. And she seems like a nice kid.'

'She wasn't quite so nice when she arrived a few days ago. Sorry. I didn't mean that. She was a bit moody when she got here but she seems to have cheered up.'

A grin tugged at Logan's mouth. 'I thought you said she didn't take after her mum?'

Evie laughed. 'I meant in looks. Perhaps she takes after her dad in that department. Do you think so?'

'Yes, I think she probably does.' He met Evie's look. 'Do you know who he is? Gran said there seemed to be some doubt.'

Evie leant closer. 'No, Logan, I don't. But I think perhaps you do.'

He nearly spilt the gravy. 'Me?' His voice was low but there was a hint of anxiety in his tone. 'How would I know? I left before anyone knew she was expecting. My dad had just died, don't forget.'

'I know. But that doesn't mean you don't know who Raven's father is.'

He stared at her for a moment. 'It's not me, Evie, if that's what you're thinking.'

'I didn't think it was,' she lied. 'But I saw the expression on your face when you realised who Raven was. You know, or at the very least, you have a strong idea.'

'OK. Let's say I did.' He leant closer to avoid being overheard. 'And I'm not saying for one minute that I do, but if I did, do you honestly think I'd say anything? I'm thinking of coming to live down this way. Severine's wrath is something I'd rather avoid, thanks all the same. Besides, I can keep a secret, Evie. Even if no one has asked me to. Don't you think you'd better go and take the rest of those orders?' He smiled and walked towards the ovens.

Logan was right. She had better go and take the rest of the orders, or they'd still be here at midnight. The identity of Raven's father had been a secret for this long; it could remain a secret a little longer.

Chapter Twenty

Snow fell thick and fast all evening. Most of the guests in the dining room glanced through the windows every so often and smiled, apart from Felicia, who seemed worried, and Tracy and Trevor Bright who were seated at the table next to her. The Brights were understandably anxious as to whether or not trains would be running. They had to get to their daughter's in Norfolk, tomorrow. Evie had no idea why Felicia was so concerned. Perhaps the woman hated snow, or perhaps she was worried that it would affect the filming of Zachary's show.

Zachary had moved to another table to discuss that with his team and as Evie went to see if they would like coffee, she asked, 'Will this weather cause you problems?'

He glanced up at her and smiled. 'Snow will

add to the authenticity and be a brilliant backdrop for the Christmas Special but it will be a problem, logistically. Driving in it is fine. Hauling cameras around in it isn't quite so appealing. Standing around in it means frozen hands, toes and bodies, even with gloves, hats, boots and layers of warm clothing. Getting a clear shot through a curtain of white flakes is another issue. At least we won't have a shortage of kids willing to play snowballs, build snowmen and make snow angels on the ground. We're plotting rough scenes now and despite the added hassle, we see it as a positive rather than a negative.'

'That's good. Would you like coffee and liqueurs here, or would you prefer to have them in the lounge where it's a little more comfortable?'

Brandon answered. 'Can we have them in the bar? I'm dying for a pint.'

'Of course. I'll make a couple of pots of coffee and put them on a table in the bar. That way you can help yourself.'

'Will the wine merchant be able to deliver in this weather?' Felicia asked when Evie approached.

So that's what she was worried about. Momentarily ignoring her, Evie turned to Tracy and Trevor Bright and smiled. 'I heard on the local radio a few minutes ago that the de-icers are out in force on the rails and that trains should be running tomorrow but may be delayed. I'll keep you posted with updates, although as it's getting on for eleven, there aren't any trains tonight, so we'll have to see what it's like in the morning. I'm sure it'll be fine.'

'You're an angel, Evie,' Tracy said. 'We'll keep our fingers and toes crossed.'

Evie turned to Felicia. 'We've had deliveries in far worse weather than this. All our stock comes from local breweries, vineyards or wine merchants. They make it here come rain or shine.'

'This is snow,' Felicia barked.

'It's a figure of speech. They make it through snow, don't worry.' As Evie headed back towards the doorway she added, 'And look on the bright side. Your champers will be extra-chilled. But it may take a while to thaw out.'

'Thaw out!'

'Must you tease her?' Zachary asked, his voice low and a crooked smile on his lips as Evie squeezed past his chair.

She bent down and whispered in his ear. 'It seems I must.' She turned away but he gently took her by the wrist as he got to his feet.

'You're no angel. You're a devil.'

'You ain't seen nothin' yet.' She laughed and tossed her hair in a coquettish fashion. He didn't release her, so she raised her brows and looked him coolly in the eye, just a hint of a grin on her face. 'Please don't manhandle the staff, sir. Not without prior permission.'

His smile widened and a second or two later, his hand slid from her wrist. Her skin tingled although his fingers had been soft against her bare flesh.

'Please accept my apologies.' He winked at her. 'I'll ask permission next time.'

He turned his attention back to his smiling team as they all stood to go to the bar. Evie noticed Brandon was staring at her and Zachary as if he knew something she didn't.

She walked through the open door into the public bar where Roland sat, staring at her.

'Is that guy bothering you,' he asked when Evie reached the bar a moment later.

'Not in the least,' she lied. Zachary was bothering her, but not in the way Roland meant. 'I thought you'd gone home. Robin arrived over an hour ago.' Exhausted, she perched on a stool and leant her forearms on the bar top.

Roland swivelled round on his stool and mirrored her action. 'I stayed for a drink. Dad's picking me up at Juniper's at eleven.'

'Where is she tonight? I texted her earlier to see if she was coming over but she hasn't replied. Oh, wait. It's that tarot thing tonight, isn't it? I was supposed to be going but then this lot happened.' Evie nodded her head back towards the throng of guests. 'Damn. It would've been fun. Did your mum go? Juniper said she might be.'

'Yes. Dad's picking them up and bringing Juniper home. That's why I'm getting a lift. Just as well in this weather.'

'Tell her to call me. I want to hear all about it.'

'Why don't you come over? Darren's out. You

can relax and wait for her to get back.'

Evie cleared her throat, reached out for a nearby towelling beer mat and wiped some beer that had been spilt on the bar top. 'Tempting. But it's a little busy here. Just ask her to call. No matter what time. Where's Darren? Did she say?'

'Working late as usual. That guy is going to work himself into an early grave.'

'Hmmm. Tell me about it. Do you know anything about his new boss?'

'Only that she cracks the whip.'

'Cracks a whip!'

Roland smirked. 'Not *a* whip, Evangeline. *The* whip. She makes him work too hard. But if you're interested in whips, I'm game.'

'Roland. You're seventeen. I'm twice your age. And no. I'm not interested in whips.' She shook her head but threw him a 'friendly' smile as she slid down from the stool.

The smile he gave her oozed sex. 'What's age got to do with anything? All that means is you may have more experience. Although I wouldn't bank on that.'

Evie was going to have to have words with Roland Green before too long. This was getting ridiculous.

'It's almost eleven. Time you went home.'

She turned away and came face to face with Zachary. How long had he been standing there? He wasn't right behind her and Roland but he was close enough to have heard some of the conversation. Roland got off his stool and hesitated, as if he wasn't sure what to do.

'See you tomorrow, Roland,' Evie said, effectively dismissing him. 'Tell Juniper to call me.'

He scowled briefly at Zachary. 'Good night, Evangeline. Night, Zachary.'

'Good night,' Evie and Zachary said in unison, and they both watched Roland walk away.

'Got a bit of a crush on you has he ... Evangeline?'

'He's seventeen. I've known him all my life. His sister is my best friend.'

'You didn't answer my question.'

'You're asking the wrong person. You'd have to ask him, not me.'

'I might just do that. At least he's got good taste.'

Evie's phone rang before she could respond to that. Glancing at the screen she saw the dancing, drunken reindeer. She smiled and waved the phone at Zachary. 'Excuse me. Got to take this.'

He nodded and stepped away.

'Hi Juniper. I was just talking about you to Roland. He's on his way. Were the cards kind?'

'Kind? They were unbelievable. Are you up? Can I come over? Any chance I can stay the night?'

'Of course you can. Are you OK?'

'I'll tell you when I get there. I can see Roly heading towards the bridge. What about this

158

weather, eh? It's incredible, isn't it? See you in five minutes.'

'I'll have a large glass of wine waiting.'

'You're an angel.'

'According to Zachary Thorn, I'm the complete opposite.'

'Oh God! He's there? Of course he's there. What's he like? Oh hi, Roly. Dad's in the car. I'm talking to Evie. Love you. Well? I asked what he is like.'

'Oh sorry. I thought you were still talking to your brother. If you run, you'll get to meet him. He's in the bar. Juniper? Juniper?' The line had gone dead.

Less than one minute later, Juniper burst in, red-faced and panting.

Chapter Twenty-One

'That man is hotter in the flesh than on TV,' Juniper said, when, a little after midnight, Evie finally managed to drag her away from the public bar and into the kitchen.

Logan had gone home and so had Robin. Everyone else had gone to bed, apart from John and Zachary and a couple of the others in Zachary's team. They were still drinking and playing cards.

Evie put a pan of milk on the hob to make some hot chocolate and Juniper flopped onto a kitchen chair, her arms sprawled across the table.

'And they're all so nice, aren't they?' Juniper continued. 'Zachary's team, I mean. Did you hear him ask me who Miranda Bradley was? He said he'd asked you but you were being very tight-lipped about it. We spent at least ten minutes discussing her knicker elastic. God! I hope he never meets her. Can you imagine how embarrassing that would be?'

'I can't see him mentioning it to her even if he did meet her. But there's not much chance of that, is there? Didn't you say she's flying out to Spain tomorrow for Christmas and New Year?'

Juniper nodded. 'If the flights aren't grounded in this weather. His family are lovely, too, aren't they? Everyone was lovely. You're lovely.'

'And you're a little bit drunk again tonight. Yes. Everyone was lovely. Apart from the harpy with two names. What is up with that woman? She's got a great boyfriend. A good job. She obviously gets paid a fortune. Did you see those shoes she was wearing?'

Juniper nodded again. 'And that dress she had on was designer. Don't ask me who because I can't afford the stuff so I wouldn't know one from another, but I can tell quality when I see it.'

'Me too. Even her jeans today were expensive. You can tell by the way they fit. Of course it does help if you've got a body like hers.'

'That's probably designer too.'

Evie grinned and handed Juniper a mug. The hot chocolate in it was topped with cream, sprinkled with chocolate shavings and rounded off with several mini marshmallows.

'So is this. Anyway. Forget about her. Tell me what the tarot cards said. What was she like? A complete con artist or the genuine article?'

'Only time will tell. Her clothes were definitely *not* designer, I can say that much. Some things she got spot on, but others, she was way off course. For instance, she knew what I did for a living and that I hate my boss. But she said I was one of three siblings. Wrong! She knew I had a boyfriend and that he did drawings of some kind. Well, he does architectural drawings so I'll give her five points for that. But here's the interesting slash weird slash I'm going to kill Darren when I see him, bit. She says that he's making plans of some sort with a woman, but that they involve me and although it means upheaval at home, I'll be happy in the end. What the hell does that mean? Does it mean I was right the other night and the bastard is 'doing a Nigel' on me? Or is this about his work and that something's going to happen? That he's going to chuck it in and the upheaval is that he won't be able to afford to pay the mortgage he took out recently to repair the roof, and we'll get thrown out. I don't know what it means, and neither did she. Oh! But she said it will come to a head at Christmas. Which is only a few days away. Then again, she said she thought his name began with the letter 'C' – and it doesn't – so I don't know if it's all a load of tosh or not. Mum says it's all nonsense and that I shouldn't take it seriously. What do you think?'

'Um. I think if you do get thrown out, you can come and stay here.' Evie smiled at her friend. 'I also think she got more wrong than she did right,

162

so I agree with your mum. On the other hand, you could tell Darren what the woman said and see how he reacts. Or, you can wait until Christmas and see what happens. But one thing is for certain. If he is cheating on you – and I still find it hard to believe, but if he is – I'll help you bury the body.'

Juniper reached out and squeezed Evie's hand. 'Aw, thanks. I can always count on you.'

'That's what friends are for.' Evie smiled again and sipped her hot chocolate.

'Ooh!' Juniper stuck her hand up in the air as if she were a child in class trying to get the teacher's attention. 'The other thing the woman said was that my brother was heading into dangerous waters and that it involved an older woman.'

Evie nearly choked on a mini marshmallow.

Chapter Twenty-Two

Snowflake Cove was a winter wonderland. Snow had continued falling during the night and by the time Evie crawled out of bed, there was at least a foot of it covering the ground. The sun hadn't yet come up, so all she could see in the darkness was the area surrounding the inn, illuminated by the lights inside the building and the fairy lights along the façade, but it looked magical.

Evie's room was in the attic, which she loved. She and Severine had shared it when they were young but as they grew up, Severine insisted on a room on the 'grown-ups floor' below. Severine was about Raven's age – fifteen – at the time and Evie was thrilled. It meant she now had one of the largest rooms in the inn, albeit long and narrow with arches and sharp angles, and a view not only of Snowflake Cove on one side, but also

Michaelmas Bay and the harbour on the other.

She also had a choice of beds. Severine insisted on a new, double bed, like the grown-ups had, so Evie got one too. But Evie asked to keep the two single beds already there. Severine soon saw the mistake she'd made. Evie could now have friends to stay, so Severine demanded bunk beds in her new room. The mattresses had been replaced over the years but the bed frames in both the attic room, and what was Severine's room, remained unchanged.

Evie peered through her window overlooking Snowflake Cove. The lights on the outdoor Christmas trees were barely visible, with only patches of pale colour shining through the blanket of white. Branches bowed under the weight of the snow and it was impossible to see the edges of the footpath leading to the bridge.

She ran with child-like enthusiasm to the window on the other side and could see the lights in Michaelmas Bay, and on the boats bobbing in the dark waters of the marina but that was all. She would have to wait until the sun came up to see more.

She opened the window just a fraction. It was chilly in her room, as usual, so it didn't make much difference. There was hardly a sound apart from the waves gently lapping at the rocks below and swishing and swooshing in and out of the inlets, one eerie cry from a gull ... and Juniper's snoring. Juniper was virtually buried beneath the duvet of the twin beds which had been pushed together to form a double, many years ago. Juniper's bed was at this end of the room, Evie's bed at the other but they were side on, enabling the occupants to lie in bed, facing one another and chattering to their hearts' content. Which is exactly what Evie and Juniper had done last night. Or should that be, early this morning, as they hadn't got to bed until after one a.m. and had still been chatting at two. Since Juniper had moved in with Darren and lived just across the bridge she no longer spent the night at Evie's, so they had made the most of it.

Evie let her friend sleep. It was only six a.m. She padded downstairs in her 'Christmas Cats' pyjamas and red fluffy, knee-length dressing gown which was covered in white doily-like snowflakes, yawning as she went. Voices and laughter wafted towards her from the kitchen. Her parents were up and so, by the sound of that cackle, was her gran. At this time? That was unusual for her.

Evie pushed the kitchen door open with her back, yawning and stretching as she twisted round. Her yawn turned into a gasp of surprise. Zachary and Brandon were sitting at the table, fully dressed, drinking coffee and eating toast. Huge grins spread across their faces and Zachary looked her up and down.

'Good morning, sweetheart,' John said. 'Goodness. You look a bit the worse for wear.'

Molly shook her head and grinned. 'Coffee?

Large, I assume.'

'Good God, Evie,' Jessie said. 'Haven't you got a mirror in your room? You look as if you've been dancing on the tiles all night.'

'Let me get my camera,' Brandon said.

Zachary didn't say a word. He merely grinned at her over the rim of his coffee mug, which was emblazoned with a snowman.

Evie pulled herself upright, sneered and tied the belt of her dressing gown tighter. 'And a very good morning to all of you,' she said, sarcastically. She gave Zachary an icy stare. 'Well? What have you got to say? I can tell from that massive grin on your face that you're dying to say something.'

He raised his brows a fraction and the grin got bigger. 'Good morning. Love the PJs. What I can see of them.'

'Go to hell.'

Molly tutted. 'That's not a very nice thing to say to a paying guest, sweetheart. And you did ask.'

'Sorry. Late night. Have you seen how deep the snow is?'

'We've been out in it,' Brandon replied. 'This place was stunning without it, but with it. Wow! It's so picturesque you'll have people flocking here to spend the holidays. I'm tempted to get the family down myself. The kids would love it.'

'You've got kids?' Evie was surprised.

'A boy and a girl. Five and eight.'

'Aw,' said Molly. 'The perfect ages at this time

of year.' She handed Evie a mug of coffee.

'I hope Tracy and Trevor Bright get back to Norfolk today,' John said. 'According to the news, it's travel chaos out there but trains are running. Just not to schedule. Speed limits have been imposed on the motorways and people are being advised to stick to the main roads where the gritting lorries have been out in force.'

'A few flakes of snow and the country grinds to a halt,' Jessie said. 'In my day a little bit of snow wasn't a major drama.'

'In your day there weren't so many maniacs behind the wheel of a lump of metal,' Evie replied. 'God. I hope the wine makes it through. Felicia will be in panic mode.' She shot a look at Zachary. 'Sorry. Me and my mouth.'

Zachary beamed at her. 'I'd already said the same before you joined us. We were planning to send out a search party if there's no sign of it by lunchtime.'

Evie grinned. 'Will this heavy snow affect your filming schedule? It's much worse than it was last night.'

'Probably. But it means we won't need the lorry load of fake snow we brought with us and that there'll be plenty of the real thing to give us the perfect backdrop. If it takes a few extra hours to set things up, so be it.'

'And you're filming the entire thing live?'

Zachary shook his head. 'We'll have live feeds from different cameras but we'll also be filming segments which will be re-sequenced and spliced together. Then we'll add transitions and special effects. It'll give the overall effect of being a live show, but parts of it will have been filmed earlier. You're welcome to come and see how it's done, but I suppose you've got better things to do with your time. Like be rude to your paying guests.' He grinned. 'I was joking. Seriously. If any of you are interested, the offer's there.'

'I'd love to see a bit of it,' John said.

'Me too,' said Molly.

Evie nodded. 'Me three. What about you, Gran?'

'I'll wait to see it 'live' from my armchair, thank you. All that standing around in the cold is not for me. Is there any more tea in that pot, Molly? I'm parched from all that laughing earlier.'

'What were you all laughing about before I came in?' Evie asked.

'Zach was telling us some of the things that can go wrong during live filming,' John said. 'Especially when animals are involved. And talking of animals. I'd better go and check on Starlight.'

'Starlight's our horse,' Evie said, to Zachary and Brandon.

'We know,' replied Zachary, with a smile. 'We met him yesterday. I suppose we'd better get started on our day too. We want to get a few shots before it gets light.' He got to his feet and looked Evie in the eye. 'We're going to start here, at the inn. This pristine snow is too good to miss and we want to get it on film before it sees too much traffic. We've got a few details to sort out but we should be ready to begin just after breakfast.'

'Too much traffic?' Evie said. 'This is Snowflake Cove. There isn't any traffic. Unless you count a couple of cars as traffic.'

'And the wine merchant going back and forth carrying all those bottles,' Zachary added, grinning. 'Being serious, once all of us, plus the guests and staff, start coming and going, leaving huge boot prints everywhere, it'll take away that aspect of remoteness. One set of footprints would be good, visually. Several, and it starts to lose the image of peace and tranquillity. See you at breakfast. Thanks for the coffee and toast, Molly.'

'You're both very welcome,' Molly said. 'Breakfast at seven?'

'If that's OK with you.'

Molly nodded. 'Perfectly OK. I'll turn the ovens on now.'

'I thought you'd had breakfast.' Evie glanced at the empty plates.

Molly tutted. 'That was just a little early morning snack, sweetheart.'

'Oh.' Evie shook her head and yawned.

Everyone started going about their business. John headed out to see Starlight, Molly attended to the ovens, and Jessie did one of the crosswords in her puzzle book.

From the corner of her eye, Evie saw Zachary

take his mobile from the pocket of his jeans hesitate for a second, then take a photo, seemingly of her.

Evie glowered at him. 'I saw that! Did you just take a photo of me? You'd better not use that in your show.'

He looked like a naughty schoolboy caught doing something he shouldn't.

'I won't. I promise.'

'Then what did you take it for?'

He met her look and held it. 'For my wallet.' He gave her an odd sort of smile, turned on his heels and strode out of the kitchen.

For his wallet? What did he mean by that?

Chapter Twenty-Three

Just how much equipment did a film crew need? Evie couldn't believe how many huge metal crates, stands, metal rods, large white screens – which were called blue – props, wires and one hundred or more other things Zachary and his team got out of the vans and cars in the car park. Thankfully, they didn't need to take it all to the inn. Her dad would have spent all day going back and forth with Starlight and the pull-along luggage cart, but it would have served him right because he was the one who had offered; they hadn't asked. It was easier, she had to admit, to load the gear into the cart, rather than the team carry it through deep snow. And the snow was deep. She hadn't realised quite how deep until she and Juniper had showered, dressed and stepped outside.

'Damn snow,' Juniper said, her boots sinking

down at about twelve inches.

'You love snow,' Evie said, giving Juniper a friendly nudge.

'Yeah. But it could've waited until tomorrow to be this deep. There's a very good chance Miranda's flight will be cancelled and the last thing I need today is to have her back in the office.'

'I don't think Gatwick got it so bad. It said on the radio that flights were delayed. It didn't say any were cancelled. We'll keep our fingers crossed. But even if she is, you've only got today and tomorrow and then you're off for a whole fortnight. Yay!'

'I can't wait.' Juniper trailed a gloved hand along one of the branches of the outdoor Christmas trees, sending a mini avalanche of snow tumbling to the blanket of white beneath. 'This looks gorgeous, but it's a shame it's covering the lights. You can only just see the colours shining through. Ooh. Talking of gorgeous. Here comes Zachary.'

'Good morning, Juniper.' Zachary gave her a smile and looked Evie up and down. 'The PJs have gone, I see. Pity.' He winked and stepped aside to let them pass.

Evie scooped a handful of snow from the tree, rolled it between her hands and threw it at him. It hit his chest with a soft thud before falling to pieces.

What had come over her? She hadn't intended to do that. Too late now though.

He gave a gasp of surprise before a smile curved his lips. 'You may regret that.'

'Really? I don't think so. That was for taking my photo.'

He grinned and shook his head. 'A fair exchange. But wait until later. I haven't had a snowball fight in years. I think it's time to put that right.'

'Is that a challenge?'

'Absolutely.'

Evie grinned. 'You're on. Juniper, Roland, Robin and Logan are on my team.'

He raised his brows. 'We're having teams?'

'Of course. But you can only have five in a team. And Felicia must be in yours.'

He burst out laughing. 'She will be pleased.'

'It'll have to be after work,' Juniper said.

'Six o'clock?' Zachary suggested.

'Oh.' Evie threw him a sarcastic look. 'I didn't realise you only work part-time. Some of us work all day and don't finish until after dinner.'

A grin curved his lips. 'Some of us start work before breakfast.'

'Some of us are far too clever for our own good. Or think they are.'

'Some us of could do with looking up the definition of 'customer care'.'

'And some of us,' Juniper said, joining in with the banter, 'have to get home, get changed, get their car out of a car park and get to work.'

'Give my regards to Miranda,' Zachary said,

still grinning.

'I'm hoping she's on her way to Spain. And if she isn't, there is no way I'm telling her about you. She'd be out here like a shot and we'd never get rid of her.'

Evie linked her arm through Juniper's. 'I'll walk with you to the car park.'

'Have a good day,' Zachary said, as they turned to walk away.

Evie glanced back at him over her shoulder. 'Shouldn't that be my line?'

He nodded. 'It should. But you seem to have forgotten to read your customer service manual.'

'Lost that long ago.'

'I'll buy you a copy for Christmas.'

'Ah,' she said, turning away. 'And here was I hoping for jewellery.'

His laughter echoed in her ears as Juniper said, 'What's going on with you two?'

'What?' Evie glanced at her. 'Nothing. We're just having some friendly banter.'

'Hmm. It seems like more than that to me. What was that about him taking your photo?'

'Yeah. That was weird. I looked awful. And I do mean *awful*. He took a photo with his phone. I was a bit concerned he might use it on the show. You know, the sort of thing where he says something about the inn they're staying at and then adds: 'The staff uniform is rather odd but the staff are efficient, eager and full of enthusiasm', and then shows the photo of me in my dressing gown

175

and PJs, hair all over the place, yawning my head off.'

Juniper sniggered. 'That would be amusing. He's not going to though, is he? Use it on the show, I mean?'

Evie shook her head. 'He said it was "for his wallet". Whatever that meant.'

'His wallet? Bloody hell, Evie. Either the man was winding you up, or he's fallen for you, big time.'

Evie darted a look back to where Zachary had been standing, but he had disappeared into the inn.

'Yes. Zachary Thorn loves Evie Starr. I don't think so, Juniper. You've seen the man. He's rich, famous, gorgeous. Has the body of a god.'

'A sex-god.'

'Yes. A sex-god. He's got a fabulous career. No doubt a spectacular home. Can have anything he wants at the snap of his fingers. And any woman, I suspect. But yes. He's obviously fallen for me, big time. I think not.'

'You're a numpty. All that stuff is irrelevant where love is concerned.'

'The guy took a photo of me when I looked like the monster from the deep. I don't call that love. I call that … potential humiliation on social media. Oh God. He wouldn't, would he? No. Forget that. I'm pretty sure he wouldn't.'

'I'm absolutely certain he wouldn't. Don't forget, Zachary Thorn has a bit of a shady past. Maybe shady is a bit too strong. But there was that incident before he left the SAS, wasn't there? People with something to hide don't usually make themselves a target for revenge by humiliating other people.'

'Oh yes. I almost forgot he had a secret. I'd rather like to know what it is, wouldn't you? And I'd still like to know why he took my photo.'

'He told you why. For his wallet.' Juniper nudged Evie. 'At least he didn't say something corny like: "I could tell you, but I'd have to kill you."'

Evie grinned. 'That's weird when you think about it. Zachary being in the SAS, I mean. He doesn't look like that sort of person, does he?'

'What sort of person? A soldier?'

'The sort who could do all that undercover, secret missions sort of stuff.'

'No, he doesn't. Ooh! I wonder if I could get him to follow Darren. Send him on a surveillance mission to find out whether my boyfriend is getting up to something he shouldn't. Take photos. That kind of thing. Although as he couldn't take a photo of you without you spotting him, perhaps that's not such a good idea.'

'Perhaps he wasn't very good. Perhaps that's why he left.'

'Maybe. But anyway, he's not in Snowflake Cove on a covert operation. He's here to film a Christmas Special. I'm so excited I could scream. We're all going to be on TV!'

Chapter Twenty-Four

Evie was not the only person to breathe a sigh of relief when the order from the wine merchant arrived. Felicia was so thrilled she insisted on opening a bottle immediately, not even caring when Evie told her that the champagne wasn't properly chilled.

'It's come on that cart via the bridge, and it's snowing outside. It's chilled. I need a bottle sent to my room, immediately. And an ice bucket, in case it does need to be chilled a little more. And two champagne glasses.'

Evie was tempted to take an empty ice bucket because the harpy with two names had not actually asked for a bucket of ice, but she thought better of it. Felicia was clearly under a lot of pressure if the woman needed champagne at ten-thirty in the morning. Why she wanted two glasses was a mystery. Her boyfriend was out filming with Zachary, and, oddly enough, her boss, Joshua was at Jane Dorset's cottage having coffee.

Jane and Joshua had bumped into one another in reception. Jane had been visiting Jessie and was on her way home. Joshua was browsing through the leaflets on the console table as if waiting for someone, or something, to arrive. He said it wasn't the wine he was waiting for when Evie enquired, and that he wasn't looking for anything in particular when she had asked him that. He was probably keeping an eye out for Jessie. Jane appeared before Evie had a chance to ask, and when Evie introduced them, Joshua offered to walk Jane home – which was very sweet and gentlemanlike. Jane invited him for coffee. That was to find out all about him, Evie was certain of it. Jessie was not at all pleased when Evie dashed into the kitchen and told her. She immediately sent a text to Jane but refused to tell Evie what it said. When Jessie's phone pinged in reply, Jessie gave a little self-satisfied smile.

'That'll show him,' Jessie said, closing her eyes and nodding off almost immediately.

Evie left her to it, returning to reception and the remainder of the day was fairly uneventful.

Zachary's parents, Juliette and Jeffrey had gone with Zachary – Jeffrey as producer of the show, Juliette to watch.

Tracy and Trevor Bright eventually managed to get a train to London and hopefully onward to

Norfolk, from there, but not at nine-thirty as they had intended. There were delays and cancellations so they waited at the inn and Evie set the train services app to notify them of updates. They finally got a train which departed at eleven-forty-five.

Logan arrived shortly after and dashed straight into the kitchen. Evie was on the landline at the time and was sure he was trying to avoid her but as he would be busy helping her mum prepare the meals, she could hardly badger him about Raven.

Joshua returned at twelve and seemed a little down-hearted, but he smiled and said he was looking forward to a delicious lunch. He was followed in by Roland, arriving just in time to serve it. Only Felicia and Joshua were having lunch, so Roland didn't have much to do.

After Raven helped Evie finish making the beds and tidying the rooms, Roland hung around Evie, making suggestive remarks. He eventually wandered off after she yawned several times and said, 'Sorry Roland, what did you say? I'm far too tired for banter.'

Juniper's message from the tarot cards might seem like nonsense but it was playing on Evie's mind. She had to do something to put Roland off and when he suggested a quick lie-down might help, she realised a rethink may be required. She asked him to go and find her dad and didn't mention that he had just gone into Michaelmas Bay to buy Molly a Christmas present. That should keep the infatuated teenager busy for a while and whilst the inn was quiet, Evie had some snow globes to wrap and arrange beneath the tree.

What would Felicia think when she opened her present on Christmas Day and found a snow globe of Snowflake Cove?

Evie grinned at the image that thought conjured up.

But what would Zachary and Joshua think?

Oh dear. Perhaps her strategy with Roland wasn't the only thing she needed to reconsider. And she was running out of time.

Her mobile rang and the dancing reindeer appeared. Either she was imagining it, or that reindeer grew more manic each day, the closer it got to Christmas.

'Hi Juniper. How's Miranda's knicker elastic? Is it on its way to Spain?'

'Fancy coming into town right now, hitting the shops for an hour, having a cocktail and still be back by six?'

'Absolutely. But I'll have to check with Mum because Dad's already out and I may be needed here. Come with me and I'll ask.' Evie hurried to the kitchen, her phone pressed against her ear. 'So I take it Gatwick didn't let you down.'

'Nope. The flight wasn't even delayed. Can you believe it? You were right this morning. Gatwick didn't get it quite as bad as we did. But the best news is that she may not be able to get back. I listened to the forecast and they said that last night was merely a sample of things to come. The whole of the UK can expect severe weather, with heavy snow, blizzards and icy conditions, not just over Christmas and the New Year, but lasting into the first two weeks of January. Isn't that fabulous?'

Chapter Twenty-Five

Evie loved shopping. Especially Christmas shopping. With the family finances looking bleak this year, she had thought she would have to tighten her belt and only buy small gifts and absolute necessities. The Thorn booking had changed that. She still couldn't go mad, but she could spend a few more pounds than expected and possibly buy a couple of little luxury gifts for her family, and for Juniper, too. Her mum had been happy for her to go into town and Juniper was waiting for her in the office doorway of Miranda Bradley Recruitment. Evie waved and the moment Juniper saw her, she turned off the office lights and locked the door.

'I've put the phones on divert,' she said, hugging Evie. 'So if Miranda calls to check up on me, she'll think I'm still at work. But let's face it, no one is going to be looking for a job at four p.m. on the last Friday before Christmas, are they? And if they are, they're bloody idiots. They should be out enjoying themselves.'

'I suppose it depends on what they did at the office Christmas party. They may suddenly need to find a new place to work. But that's their problem. You couldn't have suggested this at a better time. I need to buy presents for the guests.'

'Eh? I thought you'd got them those snow globes.'

They walked towards the High Street on a flattened path of pale grey snow. Banks of white were squashed up against the buildings but where a steady march of feet had trodden it down, it was just a thin, discoloured layer. With the temperature dropping, it was gradually turning into a sheet of ice and the soles of their boots slipped beneath them as they picked their way through the crowds, to the shops. The roads were fairly clear. Gritters had been out in force, along with the one and only snowplough in Michaelmas Bay. Zachary had been right. Traffic had ruined the picturesque look of a snow-covered town. He and his team had spent an hour filming in Snowflake Cove before heading into town as soon as that was done.

'Yes, I did. But they're spending a fortune with us. We're charging a mint for the accommodation and meals, and then they put in that wine order I told you about. We're making a massive amount of money out of that. Plus last night in the bar, money was flowing faster than the beer and liqueurs. I sort of feel they deserve more than a snow globe each, don't you?'

'It's a lovely snow globe. But yeah. You're right. But as I think I've asked before, what do you get rich people for Christmas?'

'Your guess is as good as mine. We need to look in as many shops as possible until we find the perfect gifts. And I think we should start with this one.' Evie stopped outside Michaelmas Bay Books. 'Everyone likes a book.'

'Ah, but what kind of book? I think we should start with a cocktail and make a list. It's late night opening. I know I said we'd be back by six but if we've got lots of gifts to buy we've got until eight. Some are open later. Although I suppose you have to get back to help with dinner.'

'I do. So let's say seven. OK. Cocktails it is. Then the shops.'

'If the bookshop has a book entitled 'How To Be The Perfect P.A.', I think we should get that for Felicia. That should wind her up.'

Evie grinned. 'We're looking for nice presents. We need to find something she'll like.'

'There aren't enough shops and they don't open late enough for that. Does the woman like anything?'

'I don't know. I've yet to see her smile at her boyfriend. I have no idea why he's with her. They don't seem very happy.'

Juniper pushed open the door to the cocktail

bar. 'I spoke to Darren and told him what the tarot woman said. He didn't get home until five this morning apparently. He was in bed when I went home to change and I'm not convinced he took in what I was saying. He said we'll talk tonight.'

'That's good then.'

They each ordered a Merry Mistletoe Kiss, containing vodka, Baileys, amaretto, hazelnut liqueur, cream and nutmeg, before flopping onto one of the sofas near the window. From here they could watch shoppers hurrying by, laden down with presents. Several were dragging sobbing children no doubt keen to go to Santa's Grotto, but their parents not so eager.

'It is good. But I told him I have a snowball fight to get to and that we should come over to you and talk later.'

'Are you sure that's wise? Don't you want to find out what's going on first, and then come over. Your relationship is far more important than a snowball fight.'

Juniper sipped her drink. 'Good grief. That's more of a slap than a kiss. It's yummy though.'

Evie agreed. 'We'll have to order another of these.'

'I do want to know,' Juniper said, pushing her straw up and down in the heady concoction. 'But on the other hand, I don't. What if it is bad news? What if something is going on?'

'Then surely it's better to know now. And it might not be quite as bad as you think it could. Just out of interest … what would you really do if he has been seeing someone else?'

'Oh God.' Juniper sat bolt upright. 'You think he is, don't you?'

'I didn't say that. I said what if?'

'But it's the way you said it. As if you know he is but don't want to tell me. Christ, Evie! Do you know something I don't?'

'Hello, lovely ladies. Fancy seeing you here.'

Startled by the interruption, Evie and Juniper looked up and saw Brandon Carr standing a few feet from them. No more than a second later, the door flew open and Zachary and the rest of his team piled in behind him.

'Hello!' Zachary said. 'This is a pleasant surprise. And before you say a word, we're here working. We've been told this is the best cocktail bar in town.'

'It's the *only* cocktail bar in town,' Evie replied, shooting an anxious glance at Juniper.

'May we join you?'

'Of course,' Juniper said, clearly putting on a brave face.

'Great.' Zachary smiled. 'What are you drinking? We'll get you another.'

'A Merry Mistletoe Kiss,' Evie told him.

'I like the sound of that. You haven't got any mistletoe at the inn, have you? I haven't seen any.'

'No.'

He grinned. 'I'll have to remedy that.'

He turned away and as he and Brandon headed

to the bar the whole place erupted with screams and shrieks. Zachary Thorn had been recognised. No surprise there. A crowd quickly gathered around him and his team, and Evie took the opportunity to talk to Juniper.

'I don't know anything, Juniper. If I knew that Darren was definitely seeing someone else, I would tell you. Honestly, I would. But only if I was absolutely certain. Sometimes things aren't what they seem.'

Juniper nodded. 'I know you would. I didn't mean to accuse you of keeping something from me. I'll talk to him when I get home.' She took another sip of her drink. 'I think the snowball fight might be off anyway. It'll take them all night to get away from that crowd.'

'And I think we can kiss another drink goodbye. He'll never make it to the bar.'

Chapter Twenty-Six

Evie raced into the kitchen, dumping several shopping bags by the door and kicking off her boots.

'Sorry, sorry, sorry. I know I'm late and it's seven-thirty, but my phone battery died. Did you get the text from Juniper saying we were on the way? You didn't reply and …' Evie stopped in her tracks. 'What's wrong? Has something happened?' Everyone was unusually quiet. Busy doing things, but no one was talking. That was unheard of in the Starr's kitchen. 'Mum?'

Molly threw her a wan smile. 'Sorry sweetheart. I was miles away. Did you get my text?'

'Um. No. That's what I just said. My battery died. What's up?'

'We've heard from Severine,' John said,

glancing up from an intense study of his mug of tea.

'Oh great,' Evie said, her mouth downcast. 'I mean. Oh great. That's fabulous. Um. I know she can be a pain but you're usually excited to see her. Even I'm excited to see her ... sometimes. What's wrong? Don't tell me. You told her about the Thorns and she threw a tantrum, didn't she?'

Molly had poured Evie a cup of tea without asking if she wanted one and as she handed it to Evie, she nodded.

Jessie tutted from her armchair by the Aga. 'She threw a tantrum all right. But not for the reason you think.'

'Oh? Why then? But more importantly, when is she arriving? She'd better get here soon or she might not be able to. Juniper says the forecast is horrendous ...' She let her voice trail off. Raven was sitting by the window, staring out, but she turned to face Evie and it was clear she had been crying. 'Raven? Are you OK? Will someone please tell me what's going on?'

'Mum's not coming home for Christmas.' Raven's voice was extraordinarily calm. Worryingly so. 'That's what's going on. She's spending it in Las Vegas. Why? You might ask. Because she's going there to get married. Married! Just like that. To some guy I hardly know. To some guy she hardly knows. But they're coming over for New Year. And then, guess what? We're moving to New York. Well, I'm not. I don't care

190

what she says. I'll be sixteen soon and I can choose where I want to live. And it isn't in bloody New York!'

Severine was getting married? Over Christmas? Without her daughter present? And moving to New York. No wonder Raven was crying. No wonder they were all in shock. Severine could be selfish, but she had never done anything like this. Although she had moved to London shortly after Raven was born, without telling anyone she was going until the very day she left.

'Why the rush?' It was all Evie could think to say.

'Oh, that's the best bit,' Raven said. 'I'm gonna have a baby brother or sister. Whoopee! Isn't that exciting?' She swiped at her tearful eyes. 'I suppose that is exciting. It just doesn't feel like it right now.'

This time, Evie couldn't think of anything to say. She looked from Raven to her mum and her dad and then her gran. Everyone was dumbstruck. Even Logan, who was skulking in the background, virtually blended with the cupboards.

'Married and pregnant? Bloody hell.' Evie marched over to Raven and wrapped her arms around her. Raven sung into the embrace, quietly sobbing. And Evie glanced at her mum. 'When did she call?'

'Almost an hour ago,' Molly said. 'We're all still trying to take it in. We've all hugged and had a little cry, but it doesn't seem real. Severine always comes home for Christmas.'

That was the least important issue right now. Raven must be going through hell. And yet it wasn't all bad. Raven hadn't run off to her room. That was something. Although Evie wouldn't have blamed her for a moment if she had. She was entitled to be furious over this.

'So why did Severine have a tantrum? Because you told her you don't want to live in New York?' Evie stroked Raven's hair.

Raven shook her head beneath Evie's hand. 'I didn't get a chance to tell her. As soon as she found out Zachary Thorn was staying here, filming his TV show, she threw a fit.'

'Someone told her about Zachary? After she'd just dropped that bombshell.'

'I told her,' Jessie said. 'The entire conversation was on speakerphone. She had the cheek to tell us that *Harvey* (Jessie used a shrill voice to say his name) didn't want a quiet, family Christmas. He prefers shows and casinos, bright lights and crowds of people. That's why they're in Las Vegas. Then he 'popped the question right out of the blue' (again the shrill voice, but this time imitating Severine). I lost my temper. I told her that we wouldn't be having a quiet family Christmas. And about Zachary and the show. Then she had a tantrum and said we should have told her. That if she'd known she might have persuaded *Harvey* to come. Then she slammed the phone down.'

'After you told her she and *Harvey* wouldn't be missed,' John said, but he wasn't cross with Jessie, that was obvious.

'She deserved it,' Jessie said, twisting in her seat to face the centre of the room. 'Severine thinks far too much about what she wants, and far too little about others. She's the one who hates quiet family Christmases. She always has. She does nothing but moan when she's here. All she says is that she can't wait to go home. As if spending time with us is a burden she has to bear, not something she should cherish and enjoy.'

Jessie threw Raven a look and Evie hugged her niece tighter.

Raven lifted her head. 'I did that, didn't I? When I first arrived. I'm sorry, Grammie. I'm sorry, everyone.'

'There's no need,' Evie said, and smiled as everyone said the same, or something very similar.

Raven smiled too. 'I'm gonna try really hard to make sure I don't behave that way again. I ... I don't have to go and live in New York, do I?'

'No,' Evie said. 'Not if you don't want to.'

'I'm sure we can work something out,' Molly added. 'And you're more than welcome to live here, if you'd like to and Severine agrees. But she is your mum. Don't you want to be with her?'

Raven shrugged. 'I do. I suppose. But not in New York. And not with this guy I don't really know. And I'll be in the way when the new baby arrives.'

'Of course you won't!' Molly said. 'You'll probably be a great help to your mum.'

Raven looked as if she were miles away. 'At least my brother or sister will know who their dad is. That's more than I do.'

A clatter of pans hitting the floor startled everyone, even Logan – and he was the one who dropped them.

Chapter Twenty-Seven

'Where did you disappear to?' Zachary asked when Evie went to take his dinner order. 'Are you OK? You look … distant.'

'Sorry.' Evie forced a smile. 'We've had a bit of a surprise.'

'Oh gracious,' Zachary's mum, Juliette said. 'Nothing bad I hope.

'Anything we can help with?' Zachary asked, concern written across his face.

Evie shook her head. 'Not exactly bad, I suppose, but not good either and no thanks. It's nothing we can't handle, one way or another. Um. Juniper and I left the cocktail bar when your adoring fans surrounded you.'

'I thought you had. Goes with the territory, I'm afraid.'

'Does it bother you? If you don't mind me

asking.'

He shrugged. 'Sometimes. But they're usually lovely people who just want to say hello, so it's no big deal.'

'I'd hate it. I like my privacy. Anyway, what would you all like to eat? I can recommend the Christmas Pie Pot.'

'What's that?' Zachary asked.

'It's sausage meat made locally from free range pigs, mixed with shallots, carrots and broccoli, baked in a puff pastry, homemade of course, topped with fresh cranberries. There's a cute, ceramic pie funnel in the centre to let out the steam. It's a chimney with snow and a little Santa's head coming out of it. The pie funnels are also made locally.' She grinned. 'I could've just said sausage and veg, but I'm working on my customer service skills.'

Zachary laughed. 'I'll have the Christmas Pie Pot.'

'So will I,' said Juliette. 'I think your customer service is excellent.'

'Same here,' Jeffrey added. 'Both to the pie and your customer service. I have to say, coming here took us all by surprise, but I think it's the best idea my father has had in years. We rarely feel so relaxed in the hotels where we stay. Even Felicia seems to be more at ease, and that doesn't happen often.'

'I think that's due to the champagne, not the inn, but thank you. That's lovely of you to say.

Your meals will be with you shortly. May I bring you some wine? It is yours, after all.'

Zachary chuckled. 'Roland's getting it, thanks.'

'Then I'll be back very soon. Please let me know if there is anything else I can get you.' She turned to walk away and Zachary got up and walked beside her.

'You can tell me if we're still on for the snowball fight.'

'Ah. I may have to ask for a rain check. Or snow check. Juniper may not be available and Raven may not feel up to it. That's half my team.'

Zachary leant closer. 'How about just you and me?'

'Oh I couldn't. That wouldn't be fair on you. Perhaps tomorrow.'

He grinned. 'It's the live show tomorrow. But hey! That might not be a bad idea. We could open the show with a snowball fight. Or close it with one. Brandon!' He stopped and yelled to Brandon who was sitting at a table a few feet away. 'Evie's had an idea for the show. We'll discuss it after dinner. What's the forecast for tomorrow? Has anyone checked?'

'Snow,' Felicia said, staring at her champagne glass. 'Followed by more snow. And more snow after that. Haven't you heard? We may be snowed in here? We may have to stay for New Year.' She sounded terrified at the prospect. She knocked back her glass of champagne and poured herself another.

'Snowed in.' Zachary gave Evie an incredibly and undeniably sexy look and leant in closer. 'I rather like the sound of that.'

'So do I,' Evie said, leaning towards him so that their bodies were almost touching. 'I'll let you have a note of our New Year rates, just in case.' She moved away and resumed walking towards the kitchen saying, 'I believe we have some vacancies but you'll have to be quick. Once a certain TV show is aired, people will be flocking to Snowflake Cove and paying a fortune to stay at Snowflake Inn.'

He fell into step beside her. 'As it happens, I haven't made plans for New Year. I thought I'd see how Christmas went.'

'Well, you don't want to miss the New Year's Eve firework display in Michaelmas Bay. It's similar to the Christmas Eve one which you'll see from here. But there are ten fireworks at New Year, not just five.' She grinned. 'There are leaflets on the console table in the hall detailing all the exciting festivities. But after the Christmas Eve Carols and the Boxing Day swim in the bay, you may simply want to relax over New Year. London will be so boring after your stay here.'

'That's funny. I was thinking that myself.'

Evie smiled and went into the kitchen. It was very odd, but somehow things didn't seem so bad when she was talking to Zachary. Why was that?

Chapter Twenty-Eight

Evie got out of bed and threw back the curtains. Flurries of snow drifted past the window and as the lights from the inn lit up the ground, it was obvious there had been more snow sometime during the night. After everything that happened yesterday, she had wanted an early night but that hadn't worked out and when she finally fell into bed, despite being tired, she had hardly slept a wink.

That was partly because she was concerned about Raven, and had persuaded her niece to spend the night in the attic with her. They had chatted about everything except Severine – a topic Raven was clearly trying to avoid and it had been almost midnight when Raven had finally fallen asleep.

Evie had not heard from Juniper so had sent a text at midnight. She had not liked the reply.

Despite Darren saying he would be home, he had texted to say he was running late. Juniper had a long bath, read a book and waited. He'd texted again to say he'd be home soon. At some stage Juniper had dozed off – until Evie sent her text.

Evie had phoned her and they'd chatted, but Juniper was growing ever more anxious and Evie didn't know what to say. Should she tell her best friend what she'd seen? Or should she trust Darren for a little longer and hope he was telling the truth when he said it would be settled by Christmas?

The room was chilly and Raven shivered when she woke.

'It's freezing in here. But thanks for letting me stay the night. I didn't want to be alone. I know that sounds wimpish.'

'It doesn't. I didn't want to be alone either. It was lovely having you share my room.' Evie threw on her dressing gown, grabbed Raven's from the back of a chair and tossed it at her. 'It'll all be OK, Raven. I promise you. No matter what, Severine loves you and she'll only want what's best for you. I know she will. I know I'm mean about her sometimes, but I do love her too. We'll sort something out. Trust me. And if you can't trust me, trust Mum and Dad and Gran. They're pretty formidable when they need to be.'

Raven smiled. 'I know. I trust you and I trust them. And I'm not going to worry about any of this until the New Year. I know Mum loves me and when she comes home we can sit down and talk about it. I'm hungry. And it's the TV show today. I'm really excited, aren't you?'

'Absolutely. Let's get going.'

They showered, dressed and ran downstairs. Evie wasn't surprised to find Zachary and Brandon in the kitchen and when Zachary popped back to his room to get something he'd forgotten, Evie sat next to Brandon.

'You and Zachary seem very close. Have you known him for long, or just since the show began?'

Brandon smiled. 'We've been friends for years.'

'So you knew him before he became a big TV star?' She sipped her coffee and tried to sound casual. 'What was he like before?'

'He was the same as he is now.'

'He was in the SAS, wasn't he?'

'We both were.'

That was a surprise. 'Oh. I didn't realise that.'

'No reason why you would.'

'How long for?'

'Me for ten years. Zach for eleven.'

'And ... did you leave at the same time?'

Brandon stiffened, slurped his tea and eyed Evie over the cup. 'I left a few months later. I don't know what you've heard, or think you know, but Zach did nothing wrong. In fact he did everything right.'

'Oh, I'm sure he did. I haven't heard anything – other than he resigned and then due to his heroism, he got the TV show.'

'But you want to know more?'

She shrugged nonchalantly. 'I suppose so. But not particularly. It doesn't keep me up at night.'

'That's good. It doesn't keep him up at night either. As I said, he did nothing wrong.'

'I believe you.' She smiled. 'It's obviously a sensitive subject. Sorry.'

Brandon smiled back a little warily. 'It's a classified subject. I could tell you, but I'd have to kill you.'

That old line. He was joking, of course. Wasn't he? Perhaps when the ex-SAS say it, they mean it.

She smiled more brightly. 'We wouldn't want that, would we? Let's change the subject. What's the plan for today?'

Brandon leant back in his chair. 'To get through it without too much going wrong. It snowed overnight so we'll have pristine conditions again today. We're opening the show with a montage of shots from the inside and outside of here. The Christmas trees, the reception, having breakfast in the dining room. Then outside. The frontage, the trees, the bridge, the view of the bay and the village. Then we'll cut to the live feed with Zach in Michaelmas Bay, meeting people in the town. We've got a couple of segments of him visiting the local school, followed by Santa's Grotto with some of the kids. After that we'll be live again, from the local Children's Hospice, filming Father Christmas arriving and handing out some of the presents to the kids. We'll do a piece about the importance of thinking about those less fortunate than ourselves and how even giving one pound to your local charity can make a difference because it all adds up.' He took a large swig of tea.

'It sounds really good. We're so grateful to you all for including the inn in the show, but now I feel guilty. The Michaelmas Bay Hospice for Children is far more deserving than us, obviously. We're not taking any filming time away from the hospice, are we? Because we'd all hate it if we were.'

Brandon shook his head. 'No. As awful as this sounds, the show never focuses on just one place, however deserving it may be. Joshua has made a substantial donation, so much in fact that the hospice will be able to build and equip a new wing, have a specially fitted out playground and a swimming pool added, and care for even more kids than it does now. That's what the show is all about. Making good things happen and dreams come true.'

'Oh. That's wonderful.' Evie fiddled with her coffee mug, rubbing the red nose of the cartoon reindeer on the front of it.

'It's an anonymous donation,' Brandon said, as if reading her mind. 'No names are mentioned. Just the fact that Christmas is a time for giving, but also that donations are required throughout the year, not just at Christmas. Then we have a segment on a couple of local businesses, the tree in the centre of town with all the carollers around it, singing their hearts out. Then meeting a few more people and finally, back here, where we're going to film a snowball fight – that we'd love all the residents of Snowflake Cove to be in. Then we have Zachary sitting in the lounge in an armchair by the fire, a mug of hot chocolate on a table at his side, with one of the Christmas trees in shot behind him.'

'Hot chocolate? I assumed he'd be drinking something stronger, like whisky. Or wine at the very least.'

Brandon smiled. 'It's a family show. Zach signs off by saying he hopes the only fights people have this Christmas will be snowballs fights. Tells them not to forget those less fortunate than ourselves. Wishes everyone a Merry Christmas and then he bites into one of your gingerbread reindeers. We then have a scene where it looks as if we're flying in Santa's sleigh, from the outside of the inn, back to the hospice, accompanied by Christmas music and jingling sleigh bells. We're hoping to have everyone from Snowflake Cove standing by the tree outside, all looking up and shouting, Merry Christmas. We then 'fly' over the bay and people wave from the marina and say the same, then over the town, where lots of people do the same, then to the hospice. We close with a montage of several of the kids meeting Santa and the joy on their faces, and their parents' faces, as the kids open their presents.' He grinned. 'There. You don't even have to watch the show now, do you? I just hope it all goes to plan with no major cock-ups.'

Evie smiled. 'I'll not only watch it, I'll record it.'

'I hope you're game for the snowball fight and the Merry Christmas slot. Even Felicia's agreed to be in both.'

'Really? I am surprised. You can definitely count me in.'

Chapter Twenty-Nine

Brandon need not have worried. Filming went off without a hitch. The helicopter they had hired from a nearby airfield was able to fly, thanks to almost perfect weather conditions. The sun came out and then later a light flurry of snow fell, so the crew in the air were able to get that on film. People in the marina did their bit and so did the townsfolk of Michaelmas Bay. Everyone in Snowflake Cove – including Darren – was in the Merry Christmas shot because as it was Saturday he was not working. And the team from Snowflake Cove won the snowball fight against the team from 'Thorn On Your Side'.

'We let you win for the purposes of good TV,' Zachary said, and demanded a re-match for another day.

'Any time you want to be beaten again, just let

me know,' Evie teased.

The final live shot was Zachary's sign-off in the armchair at eight p.m. that evening, and after Brandon said, 'It's in the bag' – another way of saying, 'that's a wrap', a loud cheer went up. Zachary got up from the chair and walked towards Evie who was standing in the doorway, watching. His team began clearing the place of cameras and putting the lounge back the way it was, just moments after the 'flying' scene, the montage and the credits had rolled.

'I do love these,' Zachary said, munching on the reindeer gingerbread.

'I loved the show,' Evie said.

'I think it was pretty good. It was definitely full of Christmas cheer, and that's what we were going for. Perhaps we should film it here next year.'

'Perhaps you should.' She smiled up at him. 'Are you hungry?'

He yawned. 'Sorry. I'm shattered. It's been a busy couple of days. Must be getting old. Yes, I'm hungry. And I'd quite like a pint of beer.'

Due to the filming, a large buffet was being laid out in the dining room rather than having a sit-down meal. That was partly because Zachary had said that there was always a party atmosphere after a live show and partly because all the residents of Snowflake Cove had popped into the inn to watch the action. Evie and her family knew it would be impossible to serve dinner in the dining room with such a crowd in the inn. Snowflake Cove may be small, but fitting in thirty-eight people in addition to the guests, Roland and his parents, not forgetting Robin and his family, was still a bit of a tight squeeze.

'The bar is open and the buffet will be ready in about twenty minutes. We weren't sure how long it would take your team to pack everything away ready for their departure in the morning. We'll be sad to see them go,' Evie said.

'I can't believe it's Christmas Eve tomorrow,' Zachary said, walking alongside her towards the public bar where most people had gathered. 'Your mum told me about your sister. Are you disappointed?'

'Did she?' That was a surprise. 'I'm more disappointed for Raven and my parents than I am for me. I love Severine but she drives me nuts. Christmas won't be quite the same without her though. But this year won't be our usual Christmas anyway. Because you and your family are here.'

'It's snowing again,' one of Zachary's team shouted.

'That reminds me,' Zachary said. 'I think you owe us a re-match.'

'What now?'

'No time like the present. I'll even forfeit my beer! And the guys leave in the morning, so ... unless you know we'll beat you and you're chickening out.'

'No way. You're on, mister. I'll get my team. You get yours. I'll see you outside.'

It took less than two minutes to get the teams together and everyone else either piled out to watch, or sat in the warmth of the inn to watch the fight from the windows. The moment Evie stepped outside, she was hit on the arm by a snowball wielded by Zachary and battle commenced.

Snow was falling in a soft but steady shower. There was not one breath of wind and although it was cold, it didn't feel it to Evie and obviously not to those standing around and watching. One of the crew had a shoulder-held camera and was filming it – for future shows, he said and some of the residents took videos on their phones. The sky was dark and clear, illuminated by the first quarter of a moon and a mass of twinkling stars. The Christmas lights on the inn, in the village and on the trees, together with the street lamps and the warm glow of lamps from within the inn, cast shadows and colourful reflections on the ground of white but didn't help much with visibility.

'Don't get too near the cliff edge,' Molly shouted from the doorway, hugging a mug of hot chocolate.

Evie had just made a direct hit to Zachary's head and was laughing loudly but she glanced round at her mum and followed the direction of Molly's gaze. Roland and Raven had their backs to her and were running in a straight line towards the edge. They were closer to it than they obviously realised and even Evie could only just see the steep drop-off into one of the inlets.

'Stop!' She yelled.

Roland turned his head but kept running as Raven was just inches from him and he clearly didn't want to be caught. A second later, both of them disappeared. The only indication of what had happened was a scream, a shout and two loud splashes.

Evie screamed and ran to the edge but Zachary raced past her, hesitated for a split second and dived into the channel of water between the isle and the mainland.

Only a few people had seen what had happened but Evie's screams for help soon made everyone realise something was very wrong. Pandemonium ensued and although everything happened quickly, it seemed as if it was happening in slow motion. Evie balanced precariously at the edge, peering into the darkness below. Just a few spots of colour were visible, from the reflections of the street lights and fairy lights strung between the lamp posts on the mainland but she couldn't see any sign of Raven, or Roland, or Zachary.

'Someone bring a torch,' she yelled. She had not even got the torch on her phone as she had left it indoors so as not to lose it in the snowball fight.

Brandon was by her side in seconds.

'What happened?'

She pointed madly at the water. 'They're in there somewhere. Raven and Roland and Zachary. I can't see them. Where are they? We need light. Someone bring some light.'

She was yelling and screaming and more people were running towards her. She spotted one of the team with his camera still rolling and wanted to shout at him to stop filming and to help instead. A few lights appeared from phones and other torches and Evie cursed the fact that the lighting used for filming had all been packed away.

'There!' Someone yelled.

Evie was about to dive in but Brandon squeezed her arm, told her to keep everyone back because the current was dangerous and then dived in himself. Just as Molly and John reached Evie's side, a yell went out and Evie saw Zachary in the water, lifting Raven onto the rocks. Raven looked limp and lifeless but as Brandon helped push her out of the water, she coughed. Raven was safe and so was Zachary. But where the hell was Roland?

People started running towards the path leading down to the inlet. Evie saw her dad racing down the makeshift steps, carved into the rocks, but suddenly she couldn't move. She stood and watched as if frozen to the spot. It was a circuitous route and it would take several minutes for John to get to Raven. Evie stared below. There was no sign of Zachary. Panic seized her. He must have gone to find Roland. The water would be freezing or not much above. Would he make it? Would he find Roland? The tide had been coming in so the channel was fast-flowing, as it always was when the tide turned. At least it wasn't like the rapid-filled river it often was, with waves thumping and crashing against the rocks, sending huge spumes of white into the air.

'The water isn't rough tonight,' Molly said, as if reading her mind. She hugged Evie tightly and pulled her back just a fraction from the edge. They'll be fine. I know they will. And we don't want anyone else going in there, do we?'

'How can you be so calm?' Evie croaked. 'They could die, Mum. They could be swept into the bay and drown. Or freeze to death.'

'They won't. Let's wait and see before we start panicking. Panic doesn't help anyone.'

Zachary's parents arrived, breathless and his mum was shaking, visibly. Joshua wasn't far behind.

'Is he safe? Is anyone hurt?' Joshua asked, his voice cracking with emotion and fear.

'We can't see Zachary,' Evie mumbled.

'There! I see them. They're safe.'

Another shout went out and Evie felt a thud in her chest as if her heart had stopped moments before and had just started beating again.

'Oh thank God!' Juliette said, and squeezed Evie's hand.

'We'll need blankets, hot drinks and hot water bottles.'

Evie glanced around to see Felicia who seemed to be in complete control.

'Yes,' Molly said. 'Are you all right, sweetheart?' she asked Evie. Evie nodded. 'Then

I'll go and get the blankets.'

'I'll help,' Felicia said, and then to Evie's surprise, Felicia patted her on the arm. 'It'll take a lot more than a bit of cold water to do Zachary any harm. He'll be fine. I can assure you of that.'

Juliette nodded. 'He will. Felicia's right. My son has dealt with far worse and lived to tell the tale.'

'Where's Raven?' Jessie called out, making her way slowly and carefully through the crowd. 'Is she safe?'

'She's safe.' It was Joshua who spoke. 'John and Logan are bringing her up now. Look.' He walked towards Jessie, a hesitant smile on his face and pointed towards the path. 'Everyone's safe, thank heavens. So how are you, Jessie? It's lovely to see you again after all these years, but I would have preferred to see you under different circumstances.'

She looked him up and down. 'How am I? I feel as if I almost had a heart attack. That's how I am. And I was hoping never to see you again, Joshua Thorn. Under any circumstances.'

'Ah, Jessie, my love. You haven't changed a bit.'

'Don't you use the word 'love' to me. Where's Raven? What's taking so long? We need to get her inside in the warm before she dies of pneumonia. Come along, John,' she shouted, as he and Logan appeared with Raven. 'Can't you and that boy Logan move any faster?'

213

'We're doing our best,' John said, gasping for breath.

Evie scanned the inlet and finally saw Zachary. He appeared to be giving Roland the kiss of life.

'Oh dear God!' Juniper shrieked, wrapped in Darren's arms a few feet away from Evie. 'Roly's going to be all right, isn't he? He has to be, Darren. He has to be.'

Evie suddenly remembered what the tarot card woman had said to Juniper. She'd been right. Roland had fallen into dangerous waters and it was partly because Evie had shouted at him to take care.

Chapter Thirty

'Please stop fussing, Mum,' Zachary said, smiling over his mum's head at Evie. 'That's what I want.' He winked at Evie from his chair beside the fire in the lounge. 'And the pint.'

Evie smiled back. 'We were all worried sick. Your mum isn't fussing. She simply wants to be sure you're all right.'

He shook his head. 'I'm fine. I've been fine for the past half hour and I'll be even better once I've had a pint of beer and everyone stops hanging around, giving me those worried looks. How're Raven and Roland?'

'They're OK. Roland's in one of the guest bedrooms and his parents are with him. We've called a doctor just in case he's got hypothermia or something, but he seems fine. Raven is being hugged to death by Mum and Dad, and lectured by

Gran. Lovingly, of course. Raven and Roland are both eager to thank you for saving their lives, but we've told them it can wait.'

'No need for thanks. I did what anyone else would have.'

'I didn't dive in to save them and neither did anyone else. Only you and Brandon.'

'That's because most people are incapacitated by shock. Brandon and I are trained to react.' A cloud seemed to form over his eyes. 'Although sometimes I don't get it right.'

'Are you hungry, Zach?' Juliette asked.

'Starving.'

'I'll get you some food.'

Evie put a hand on Juliette's shoulder. 'I'll get it. You stay here.'

Juliette shook her head. 'Thank you, Evie, but I want to check on Jeffrey and Joshua. They've had a nasty shock too. Jeffrey has accompanied his father to Joshua's room. This boy of mine will be the death of us all with his constant heroism.'

Zachary tutted. 'Mum.' He shook his head and Juliette shrugged. It was as if they had had this conversation many times before and Zachary didn't like it.

Juliette smiled and left the room.

'Hey, Zach,' Brandon said, returning to the chair opposite Zachary, having called his wife from the privacy of his bedroom, to tell her what happened. 'You'll never guess what. We're on the news. Eddie filmed the whole thing and it's been

216

picked up by every channel, so it seems. Even abroad.'

'Damn,' Zachary said. 'Oh well. I suppose it's more publicity for the show.'

Evie laughed. 'You're both heroes and all you can think about is the show!'

Brandon smiled. 'We ex-SAS boys take this stuff with a pinch of salt.'

Zachary threw him a look but didn't say a word.

Robin came in with a plate of food and handed it to Zachary. 'Your mum sent this. Have you seen we're all on the news? Well, mainly you and Brandon and Raven and Roland but there're shots of all of us. And the snowball fight. And Raven and Roland disappearing over the edge. It's all very dramatic. And not all grainy like these things are when filmed by someone on a phone. Because it was filmed by one of your team. You'll be given a medal at this rate.'

'He's got medals,' Brandon replied.

Again Zachary threw him that look before tucking into the food Robin had brought, as if he hadn't eaten for a year.

Chapter Thirty-One

'Merry Christmas Eve,' Evie said, dashing into the kitchen at breakfast the following morning already dressed. 'How is everyone after all the excitement of yesterday? Raven's still fast asleep but she's fine because I checked. Twice. Before coming down.'

'Roland's fine too,' Molly said. 'I took Sylvie a cup of tea and she was still in her son's room but she said he slept like a log. And of course the doctor gave him the all clear when he was here last night.'

'Any sign of Zachary?' Evie pulled out a chair and sat at the table.

'Not yet,' John said. 'But I heard movement in several of the rooms, including his, about half an hour ago, so I'm sure he's fine. His team are leaving shortly and they'll be having breakfast early so they'll probably be down any minute.'

'Oh. I'd better sort out the tables then.' Evie jumped up.

'No need,' Molly said. 'Logan did them last night before he left.'

Evie plopped back down. 'Excellent. What's the weather like?' She stretched her neck to glance outside through the window. 'Too dark to see. I forgot to look when I was in my room.'

'It's not snowing,' John said, 'and it feels a little warmer but the forecast says fine weather this morning, followed by a sudden drop in temperature later and heavy snow with blizzard-like conditions on the way by evening.'

'So it might actually snow on Christmas Day?'

'There's a very strong likelihood it will.'

'The turkeys are arriving this morning,' Molly said.

Evie laughed. 'Sorry. I had an image then of a parade of turkeys strutting across the bridge.'

Molly smiled. 'You're in a jolly mood.'

'I'm always jolly.'

'But more so today.'

'That's because three people I care about nearly died last night. It makes one realise how wonderful it is to be alive, don't you think?'

'Three people? Oh, you mean Zachary, too. Well, from what I hear, I don't think there was any question of him dying. The things that young man has been through beggar belief.'

'How do you know what he's been through,

219

Mum?'

'I spent several hours chatting with Juliette. She's had a lot to deal with, not that you'd know it from the way she talks of it. She did say she thought her worrying days were over when Zachary left the army, but he keeps finding himself in life-threatening situations. Mind you, he seems to handle them without a problem except …'

'Except?' Evie queried. 'Except what?'

'Except for the time he lost a man. Juliette says he blamed himself.'

'Did she say what happened?'

Molly shook her head. 'Only that last night must have brought back memories, so it must have involved water, I suppose.'

'I don't think they're allowed to talk about it, are they?' John said. 'Wasn't it classified?'

'Merry Christmas Eve,' Logan burst in, smiling from ear to ear.

'Another one who's extra jolly,' Molly said. 'Morning, Logan. Merry Christmas Eve to you too.'

'Have you seen the papers? They must have changed the front pages at the last minute. Look at this.'

He spread two different tabloid papers on the table. Both had photos of Zachary and Brandon on the front. One had 'Ex-SAS to the rescue' as a heading. The other had 'Second time lucky' with an additional photo of Zachary in military uniform. He looked different but not by much.

Logan poured himself some coffee from the fresh pot Molly had put on the table. 'It says that last night could have ended with a different result. That the last time Zachary dived into freezing waters to save a man, he came up empty. The man died. It's all over social media, too. Hashtag Zachary Thorn, is trending.'

'What?' Evie shrieked, and grabbed the paper.

'So much for classified information,' John said, shaking his head. 'I don't think you should read that, sweetheart. Better to leave such things alone. If Zach wants anyone to know, I'm sure he'll tell them himself.'

Evie looked at the headline. Her dad was right. This was a bit like reading someone's diary. She wouldn't do that without their permission. It didn't feel right. Zachary had hesitated at the edge for a fraction of a second last night. Had this previous occasion flashed through his mind? No matter how much she would love to know the truth, did it really matter? And was she likely to get it from a newspaper story, no doubt put together in a rush and possibly dramatized to sell more copies? It was Zachary's secret and she had no right to pry. She pushed the paper away.

Zachary was a hero. She had witnessed it with her own eyes.

Chapter Thirty-Two

'I suppose you've seen the papers and social media,' Zachary said when Evie went into the dining room to serve him breakfast.

The tables had been sprinkled with snowflake confetti to give them a festive touch and for a centrepiece, each table had a fruit sculpture of sorts. Varieties of fresh fruit had been peeled, sliced, shaped and stacked, layer upon layer until – Lego-like – they resembled a Christmas tree.

'I saw them. But I didn't read them and I haven't checked anything else this morning.'

'Oh?' He seemed surprised.

'It didn't feel right, somehow, to read about you like that.' She shrugged. 'I can't really explain.'

'Nor can I. Explain, I mean. It's supposed to be classified. But I want you to know, I did everything I could to find him. Everything. He was gone and there was nothing I could do.'

'The man who died, you mean? I don't doubt it for a moment. I saw you last night.'

'I hesitated last night.' He shook his head and dragged one hand through his hair. 'It could have gone bad very quickly.'

'It didn't. Raven is singing carols in the kitchen. Roland is scoffing down breakfast in bed. It's Christmas Eve and all is right with the world. OK. Maybe not all. But in Snowflake Cove it is. Or it will be. What time is your team leaving? Blizzards are forecast.'

'In about an hour. After we've had breakfast.'

'Then I'd better hurry up and serve them. Merry Christmas Eve.'

He smiled. 'Merry Christmas Eve to you, too.'

Evie dashed to and fro and within fifteen minutes everyone was tucking into bacon, eggs, mushrooms, beans, tomatoes, and toast, all washed down with fruit juice, coffee and tea. Raven helped serve, after running over to Zachary, hugging him and giving him a kiss on the cheek.

'Thank you so, so much for saving my life! I've seen it on the news and I wouldn't have dived into that water for anyone.'

Evie laughed. 'So don't fall in because she won't be coming after you. And neither will I.'

Zachary grinned. 'That's good to know. I'll take extra care the next time we have a snowball fight. You were losing, by the way.'

'Rubbish!' Evie said. 'You just don't know when you're beaten. What are your plans for today? Once your team have left. Just lazing about doing nothing as usual, I suppose.'

His grin broadened. 'Doing some Christmas shopping. I haven't done any. I forgot today was Sunday. The shops will be open, won't they?'

'Typical man. Leave it all until the last minute. I should think they'll be open. If they are, they'll be packed with men. We women will all be home, wrapping presents and sipping sherry with Michael Bublé. Sadly, he'll only be on the radio, not actually here. If he were here, the presents could go to hell.'

'So you like Michael Bublé?'

'Doesn't everyone?'

'Yes. I'm his biggest fan.'

'Excellent! Because I've got you his entire collection for Christmas.'

Zachary laughed. 'I'd rather have one of those Merry Mistletoe Kisses with you … in the cocktail bar in Michaelmas Bay.'

'I'll get in line with the rest of your adoring fans.'

'Does that mean you're an adoring fan?'

She eyed him up and down. 'Of course. You saved my niece's life. I'll love you forever. The Merry Mistletoe Kisses are on me.'

'Now that conjures up an image I rather like. In more ways than one. I must remember to get that mistletoe. But right now, I'd better say goodbye to my team. I'll see you later, Evie.'

Chapter Thirty-Three

After she had also said her goodbyes to Zachary's team and given them all their beautifully wrapped snow globes, Evie and Raven stripped the beds of the now vacant rooms and cleaned and vacuumed throughout. Zachary and his family, including Joshua, together with Felicia and Pete, went into Michaelmas Bay for Christmas shopping. Evie and her family stopped for lunch and then she helped in the kitchen, took delivery of the turkeys, iced the Christmas cakes and washed the chestnuts ready for roasting over the fires, later.

She wrapped the presents, tossing the one for Severine to one side and took them downstairs to go beneath the tree.

Zachary and his family returned around two and Zachary went with John to get more logs. If the weather was going to be really bad, the last thing they wanted was to run out. When Zachary learned that they actually had to cut down the trees from Michaelmas Great Wood, he seemed even more keen, not less. Evie teased him about it later.

'You've clearly been having a few of those Merry Mistletoe Kisses without me,' she said. 'There is nothing exciting about chopping down trees in the cold and snow. You must be mad – or drunk.'

'It was fun. It's been a long time since I did anything like that. As for the Merry Mistletoe Kisses, I can't contemplate having even one without you,' he said. He grinned and grabbed her hand. 'Come with me.'

'I'm busy,' she said.

'It'll only take one minute. Maybe two.'

He led her into reception and there, just inside the front door, was a huge bunch of mistletoe. Evie tried to back away, but he held her hand a little tighter and stopped beneath the hanging bunch.

'May I please manhandle the staff?'

His eyes twinkled and the sexiest grin Evie had ever seen, spread across his lips.

'I told you I would ask the next time. But even if the answer is no, I'm afraid I may have to veto it. This is tradition, after all.'

Evie raised herself on to her tiptoes and gave him the briefest peck on the lips that she possibly could, but instead of letting her go, he held her tighter.

'I take it that's a yes,' he said.

'That was a kiss.'

'No it wasn't. At least not the sort of kiss I had in mind. That was merely a taste of things to come.'

He pulled her into his arms before she knew what was happening but the second his mouth covered hers, she didn't want to pull away. When they finally eased away from one another, their breathing was deep and fast, their chests were rising and falling and their faces were as red and hot as the fire burning in the hearth.

'Wow!' Evie said, trying to catch her breath. 'That wasn't a minute or two. That was more like five.'

'That was pretty wonderful. May I manhandle you again, please?'

'You can manhandle me as often as you like.' She leant into him and looked up into his eyes. 'I'm working on my customer service.'

'Evangeline!' It was Roland and he sounded as if he was being strangled. 'So that's the way it is, is it?'

She shot a look in his direction. 'It is, Roland. I'm sorry.'

Roland shrugged. 'That's OK. The man did save my life. But if it doesn't work out, you know where I live.'

'What's that?' Roland's mum, Sylvie asked, coming into view a moment later.

'Nothing, Mum. We're going home, Evangeline. But I'll be back later to work.'

'Are you sure you're feeling up to that? You

don't have to. We'll be able to cope, as the number of guests has halved.'

'No. I'm up to it. See you later.'

Zachary waited until they had left. He then pulled Evie back into his arms. 'Now where were we? Ah yes. We were working on your customer service.' And he kissed her again. For a lot, lot longer.

Chapter Thirty-Four

Snow had been falling heavily all afternoon and the winds were whipping up as carollers gathered around the tree on the mainland of Snowflake Cove. There was no moon, but even if there had been, it would have been hidden by the mass of thick cloud. Aside from the villagers' homes, the only other illumination was from the street lights and the fairy lights strung between the lamp posts. Zachary had his arms wrapped around Evie, and Darren and Juniper were beside them. Raven and Robin stood smiling at one another just in front of Evie and Zachary and Evie couldn't help but wonder if Raven had switched her affections, which was probably just as well. Severine had eventually phoned back, having seen on the news what happened to her daughter. It had been shown worldwide due to the popularity of Zachary's TV show.

The first thing she asked, after checking Raven was OK was why her daughter had been running after Roland Green? When Molly told Severine that Raven had a bit of a crush on the lad, Severine threw the worst tantrum they had ever heard. That couldn't happen, she had shrieked. They must make sure Raven stayed away from that boy. And so it went on until for once, Molly had been the one to hang up on Severine.

'Perhaps if you were here with your daughter instead of getting married to someone you hardly know, and in Las Vegas of all places, you could tell Raven yourself. Merry Christmas, Severine.'

The rest of the family had been stunned. But it was the right thing to do.

Evie was surprised by Zachary's singing voice as they joined in with the carollers, and even more surprised when she saw Jessie walking slowly across the bridge, side by side with Joshua. Every so often he reached out to try to take her arm in his but she pushed it away and Evie giggled as she could imagine what her gran was saying to him. Still, at least she was now talking to the man.

Juniper hadn't mentioned if she'd spoken to Darren or not yet. So much happened yesterday that Juniper probably felt it wasn't the right time to find out if her boyfriend was cheating. It was Christmas Day tomorrow and Darren had promised Evie it would be sorted out by then. She hoped it would be. And she hoped it would have a happy ending. She smiled at her friend and her friend smiled back. Then, suddenly, Juniper's face turned pale, her eyes grew wide and her mouth fell open.

'Dad?' She croaked. 'Oh my God. It is you!'

Evie glanced around, wondering why Juniper would behave in such a way towards her dad but the man walking towards Juniper and the crowd was not Peter Green. He was tall and broad with olive skin and hair as black as a Raven's wing.

A Raven's wing!

Evie's shocked gaze shot to Raven and back to the man. The man she now realised she had seen photos of many years ago. The man who had disappeared without a word almost sixteen years before. It was Roggero Tazzeone – Juniper and Roland's biological birth father.

And now Severine's secret was out. He wasn't just Juniper and Roland's father – he was also Raven's. The likeness was undeniable and he was looking at Raven as if he knew exactly who she was.

So Severine had had an affair with the father of Evie's best friend. Somehow, Evie wasn't as surprised as she should have been. No wonder Severine had thrown a fit about Raven having a crush on Roland. Now it all made sense.

Chapter Thirty-Five

Christmas Eve hadn't gone quite the way anyone expected, not least Evie. Once the news was out that Roggero Tazzeone was back and that he was Raven's dad, all hell broke loose. Sylvie was understandably not pleased. Juniper was in a state of shock but she did say the tarot woman had got another thing right. The woman had said Juniper was one of three – and she was ... Raven was her half-sister. So now she was even more concerned about Darren, although she was thrilled to have a sister – especially a sister who was also Evie's niece.

Molly and John were mortified. Sylvie and Molly were good friends. How could Severine have done such an awful, deceitful thing? Now no one was looking forward to Severine coming home for New Year.

By the end of the evening, when everyone stood outside on the terrace, watching the fireworks in Michaelmas Bay, it wasn't the peaceful and tranquil Christmas Eve, roasting chestnuts on the fire, playing board games and charades and drinking hot chocolate with Baileys and eating mince pies, that the Starrs had planned.

The astonishing thing was though, when Roggero Tazzeone said that he had seen two of his children almost drowned and the third sobbing at the edge of the isle, on the news and had rushed to the airport and caught the first available flight to England and then spent hours getting to Michaelmas Bay by train, to come and see them, Juniper and Roland – and even Sylvie, to a certain extent – forgave him for abandoning them.

And Raven, who had no idea he was her dad until now, was so excited to finally meet him that she didn't care he had abandoned her mother after Severine told him she was pregnant. He may not be the best of fathers – but at least she had a father she could name. Somehow, that made a difference.

Molly and John let him stay at the inn and he spent most of the night talking to Raven. Evie hadn't heard him ask once about Severine though so how this would all turn out was anyone's guess.

'Well,' Evie said to Zachary as he kissed her good night around one in the morning. 'I bet you didn't expect your Christmas to be this exciting, did you?'

'No,' he said. 'And I'm looking forward to

next Christmas already. What do the Starrs – and the stars – have in store for the Thorns, I wonder? Did you see Pops and your gran are speaking?'

'Only just. Let's see what tomorrow brings on that score.'

Chapter Thirty-Six

Christmas Day brought more snow. There had been blizzards overnight but now there were light flurries and every now and then, the clouds parted and the early morning sun shone through as if it too, wanted to wish everyone in Snowflake Cove a Merry Christmas.

Evie was in the kitchen helping her mum and every time the kitchen door swung open, she looked up hoping to see Zachary. After the incredible kisses they had shared, her dreams last night had been filled with thoughts of him. And not merely thoughts. She had never experienced such excitement and longing for any other man. Several times she woke up and had to suppress the urge to go to his room in the middle of the night. This morning, in the shower, all she could think of was being in his arms. Did Zachary feel the same?

Or was she hoping for a miracle where he was concerned?

Despite the late night, Raven was up at the crack of dawn, had made coffee and tea for everyone, had wished them a Merry Christmas, with a beaming smile and had gone for a walk with her dad. Evie wasn't sure what surprised her the most. That Raven was up and out before the sun had barely risen. Or that she was happy to go for a walk in the snow, with the temperature not much above freezing. Or that she had done all of these things with joyful enthusiasm. What a difference a dad makes. Evie just hoped Roggero would stick around this time. Although with Severine coming home for New Year, things might get even more interesting, to say the least.

Breakfast today was smoked salmon and champagne, so there wasn't any cooking, as such – which was just as well because they'd given Logan the morning off. He, together with his mum and his gran would be joining the Starrs and their guests for Christmas dinner, and he'd be helping later with that.

'Well, you were right, Dad,' Evie said, pouring each of her family a glass of champagne. 'You said everything would sort itself out by Christmas and I think we can safely say it has.'

'Let's have a toast to that,' John said.

They raised their glasses but before the toast was made, Juniper burst into the kitchen, crying.

'Evie!' Juniper sobbed. 'I had to come and tell

you right away. Oh. Merry Christmas.'

'Forget Merry Christmas, Juniper. What's wrong?' Evie set her glass down on the table and ran to her friend. 'Is this about Darren? Has something happened?'

Juniper nodded frantically. 'I don't know what to say. I'm ... I'm so happy I could cry.'

Jessie tutted. 'You are,' she said. 'Will someone give the girl a drink. And a tissue. She clearly needs both. Then tell me what on earth is going on? I'm not sure this old heart of mine can take much more drama. Out with it, Juniper. Is your boyfriend having an affair or not?'

'He's not! He's ... he's had a kitchen designer come around and he's having an extension built to make room for a new kitchen ... and he's been working all hours to pay for it!'

'No wonder you're crying,' Jessie said. 'No one wants a new kitchen for Christmas. That's as bad as getting a new vacuum or something. Only bigger.'

'But I want a new kitchen! I've wanted a new kitchen since the day I moved in. I spend hours scanning magazines and dreaming. This is the most wonderful gift I've ever had. The plans were wrapped in a Christmas Cracker and they're perfect. It's the kitchen of my dreams. But I can change any of it if I want. I love him so much. I must get back and tell him. I only popped over whilst he was in the shower. Merry Christmas ... again!'

She was still sobbing when she ran out, almost knocking Zachary over in her haste. She stopped. Kissed him on the cheek, wished him a Merry Christmas and was gone.

'That girl has a strange idea of what a Christmas present should be,' Jessie remarked.

Zachary handed her an envelope. 'Pops asked me to give you this. He says he would love to talk to you and he's in the lounge if you're willing to.'

Jessie frowned. 'I talked to him yesterday. And the day before.'

'Not about what he wants to talk about, apparently.'

Jessie scowled. 'What's this?'

'An envelope,' Zachary said.

'Don't get smart with me you young whippersnapper. What's in the envelope?'

'I honestly have no idea.'

Evie laughed. 'Open it and see, Gran.'

'You open it.' She handed it to Evie.

Evie smiled and ripped it open. Her heart skipped a beat and her eyes shot to Zachary and then to Jessie. 'It's an I.O.U., Gran, made out to you. And I don't think I've ever seen so many zeros in my life. Look!'

'So,' Jessie said, her eyes narrowing as she read the note. 'He's paying his dues, at last. I'll talk to the man. But I need more champagne first. A magnum of the stuff, at the very least.'

'What dues?' John asked, taking the piece of expensive-looking notepaper from Evie and choking when he saw the amount. 'Why would Joshua Thorn owe you this much money, Mum? Why would he owe you any money for that matter?'

'Because he does. That's why,' Jessie said. 'He cheated William out of it many, many years ago. I'll tell you all about that another time.' She looked up at a photo hanging on the wall, of her and her long-deceased husband, William and smiled as if he was looking down at her. She raised her glass and blew him a kiss.

They all knew there was no point in pressing the subject. Jessie Starr was as stubborn as a mule and if she didn't want to talk about something, that was that. They would simply have to wait until she was ready to share this secret with them.

Zachary walked over to Evie and kissed her on the lips. 'Merry Christmas, Evie,' he said.

'Merry Christmas,' she replied, still a little stunned. 'Why has your grandad given my gran an I.O.U. for one million pounds, Zachary? One. Million. Pounds!'

'Well, it's better than a new kitchen,' Molly said.

Zachary smiled. 'I have no idea what that means, and I have no idea why Pops has done that. But it's his money and he can do whatever he likes with it. Where's my Michael Bublé collection, that's what I want to know?'

'It's under the tree. But you can have this present now.' She grinned at him. 'It would serve you right if I really had bought you Michael Bublé's greatest hits. But I haven't.'

She handed him a beautifully presented gift and he carefully unwrapped it.

'A snow globe,' he said, seemingly genuinely pleased. 'A snow globe of Snowflake Cove. It's beautiful, Evie. Thank you.'

'I bought one for everyone, as a memento of their stay, so that every time you look at it, you'll remember Snowflake Inn.'

'I don't need to remember it,' he said. 'I'm planning to visit frequently. In fact, I'd like to book a room from the day after Boxing Day until at least the 6th of January when I have to return to work.'

'Hmm,' Evie said, excitement bubbling inside her – and not from the champagne. 'I'll have to see if we have any vacancies. Now that we've been on TV everyone wants to come and stay.'

'In that case,' he said. 'We should make it an ongoing booking. That way, I can pop back whenever I like.'

'Wonderful,' Evie said. 'We'll even give you a discount in that case. Merry Christmas, Zachary. I hope you get everything you wished for.'

'Merry Christmas, Evie.' He took his wallet out and showed her a photo. It was the one he'd taken of her. 'I think I already have. Now would you like to see your present?'

Evie beamed at him. 'If that photo in your wallet means what I think it does, then you're my

Christmas present, Zachary Thorn. I have just remembered what you told me about your grandad and my Gran's photo.'

He smiled and his eyes lit up as he looked down at her. 'I'll be the gift that keeps on giving, Evie – if you'll let me. And I won't just be your Christmas present. I hope I'll be your Christmas future, too. But I do have another Christmas present for you. It's under the tree. Shall we go and get it?'

'We need to go via the mistletoe. This member of staff needs manhandling again. And she also needs to show you that she's improved her customer care skills no end. Customer satisfaction is now guaranteed.'

He glanced around the room and grinned before whispering in her ear, 'I like the sound of that. But we don't need to stand in the hall, do we?'

She raised herself up to whisper into his. 'Who said anything about the hall? It just so happens there's a bunch of mistletoe in the attic.'

'The attic?'

'Yes. Which also happens to be my room. I'd quite like to manhandle one of the customers, if that's all right with you?'

'All right with me? That sounds absolutely perfect.'

Evie took his hand in hers and they sneaked out of the kitchen, seemingly without any of the others noticing. Or perhaps they were all too polite to comment. Or still in shock over the amount of Joshua's I.O.U.

Evie didn't really care. She wasn't sure what the future would bring but she knew two things for certain.

Christmas really was a time for miracles and magic.

And the future was looking very bright for the Starrs.

The End
MERRY CHRISTMAS!

Coming soon

Book Two in the Michaelmas Bay series. See my website for details.

A Note from Emily

Thank you for reading this book. A little piece of my heart goes into all of my books and when I send them on their way, I really hope they bring a smile to someone's face. If this book made you smile, or gave you a few pleasant hours of relaxation, I'd love it if you would tell your friends.

I'd be really happy if you have a minute or two to post a review. Just a line will do, and a kind review makes such a difference to my day – to any author's day. Huge thanks to those of you who do so, and for your lovely comments and support on social media. Thank you.

A writer's life can be lonely at times. Sharing a virtual cup of coffee or a glass of wine, or exchanging a few friendly words on Facebook, Twitter or Instagram is so much fun.

You might like to join my Readers' Club by signing up for my newsletter. It's absolutely free, your email address is safe and won't be shared and I won't bombard you, I promise. You can enter competitions and enjoy some giveaways. In addition to that, there's my author page on Facebook and there's also a new Facebook group. You can chat with me and with other fans and get access to my book news, snippets from my daily life, early extracts from my books and lots more besides. Details are on the 'For You' page of my website. You'll find all my contact links in the Contact section following this.

I'm working on my next book right now. Let's see where my characters take us this time. Hope to chat with you soon.

To see details of my other books, please go to the books page on my website, or scan the QR code below to see all my books on Amazon.

Contact

If you want to be the first to hear Emily's news, find out about book releases, enter competitions and gain automatic entry into her Readers' Club, go to: https://www.emilyharvale.com and subscribe to her newsletter via the 'Sign me up' box. If you love Emily's books and want to chat with her and other fans, ask to join the exclusive Emily Harvale's Readers' Club Facebook group.

Or come and say 'Hello' on Facebook, Twitter and Instagram.

Contact Emily via social media:
www.twitter.com/emilyharvale
www.facebook.com/emilyharvalewriter
www.facebook.com/emilyharvale
www.instagram.com/emilyharvale

Or by email via the website:
www.emilyharvale.com

24868693R00151

Printed in Great Britain
by Amazon